SUMMER OF THE CICADAS
A NOVEL

COLE LAVALAIS

WILLOW BOOKS

Detroit, Michigan

Summer of the Cicadas

Copyright © 2016 by Cole Lavalais

Editor: Randall Horton
Cover art: Jennifer Everett
Cover design: Bryant Smith

ISBN 978-0-9961390-4-5
LCCN 2016936354

Willow Books, a Division of Aquarius Press
PO Box 23096
Detroit, MI 48223
www.WillowLit.net

Printed in the United States of America

For Viola, Vanessa, Lola, Daisy, Roberta & Elizabeth

CHAPTER ONE

She'd witnessed the raised ridged skin of the girls at school. Accidental glimpses in the locker room after track practice, quick changes in bathroom stalls, long sleeves in the midst of Chicago's unpredictable Indian summers; all futile attempts to keep private pains hidden. Vi called them the Carvers: girls who engraved inscriptions of unhappiness into their skin. Most of the Carvers cut casually. Slipping out the razors only for the big stuff; unanticipated Ivy League rejection, or a bad break-up with the prom king. Then there were the heavy hitters. Every unreturned phone call or misinterpreted side-eye, every slight, no matter how minute, recorded in welted vines of discontent riding up inner thighs and forearms and abdomens; cloistered havens hidden from public scrutiny. But Vi wasn't a Carver, couldn't care less about the interworkings of her high school or the leagues of Ivy that would follow. The only thing Vi cared about was Cecilia, and she was doing no more than Cecilia would do for her. If anything, Vi saw herself as a hero, not some mentally-stunted, hormone-filled, insecure teenie-bopper. A hero. Cecilia needed her. She could no more exist without Vi, as Vi could exist without her. The doctors didn't understand. Couldn't see the cancerous lumps, so cancerous lumps didn't exist, but Vi knew they existed. After the third oncologist insisted, with a sweetness reserved for crazies and/or toddlers, a biopsy was downright unnecessary, Vi knew she would have to take life into her own hands. As surely as the doctor's patronizing voice dissipated alongside all sound, she knew. The sudden deafness didn't surprise her. She read in biology class the human body could only take so much before it started to shut down. It just so happened her hearing went first. She saw it as a sign. If she didn't do something soon, it would only be a matter of time. A week later another sign crawled into her ear in the middle of the night—a newly awakened cicada. Its vibrant croaking the first sound she'd heard in days. The bulbous beetle had fought its way out of a nearly two decade-long hibernation to tell her the only way to save herself was to carve out the cancer. The wimpy razors favored by the Carvers wouldn't be suitable for the task in front of her. She sharpened Cecilia's preferred poultry knife until the mildest touch to its edge yielded a perfectly formed line of blood across her fingertip. The bathtub sat half-filled with hot water. Cecilia would be home soon, just in time to take her to the hospital. Just in time to save her life, but not her breasts. Her legs shook as she stepped into the bathroom. Her once singular cicada had multiplied. Discarded husks littered the sidewalks and front porches up and down the street, and at this moment, they all seemed to be nesting outside of her bathroom window, raising their voices in unison as if at the beckoning of some sort of invisible miniature conductor. While Vi welcomed the initial reawakening of sound, this legion of croaking bugs unnerved her. She slammed the window shut, quelling, if not silencing, the raucous concerto, before lowering herself into the water. The first cut didn't hurt. She would be able to go through with it. The threat to her very existence would be removed for good. She cut again. Her skin parted from her body exposing a thin cottage cheese like white layer on the inside of her brown skin; her blood, more brown than the slasher-movie red, pulsed out of the gash as if it had been waiting for a chance to escape; the sweet smell of copper filled the steamy bathroom. Raising Cecilia's knife to finish what she'd started, her hand juddered. She had to finish. The cicadas' timber grew deeper, richer, and she really needed them to shut the fuck up.

   —*Shut the Fuck Up!*

But they didn't and the shaking became more pronounced. She sliced again anyway. This time on the underside, forming a crooked bloody C around her left breast. More blood; followed by vomit. One more cut and she would be free. Her genetic predisposition thwarted. She attempted to raise her arm, but her arm did not move. Her body parts were turning against her. Fight or flight. She'd read about that in biology, too. Her body must've been in fight mode, but who was it fighting? Her blood clouded the water—her submerged limbs no longer clearly distinguishable. Vi couldn't lift either arm, and her eyelids felt heavy. She wondered what time it was? Cecilia should be home soon. She hoped she'd cut enough. Vi waited for the familiar sound of her mother pulling her car into the garage, but only the hum of the vibrating cicadas remained, and even that soon drifted away, leaving only a bed of pure blackness. All of her parts relaxed into it, and she no longer felt afraid.

CHAPTER TWO

The air in Tallahassee didn't move. In Chicago she'd fought to stay on her feet. Lake Michigan's winds blew hardest through the South Side, pushing one way and then the other, rendering movement agentless. But in this new place, nothing pushed. Except of course, the momentum of the other deplaning passengers. But that was temporary. These people would eventually collect their suitcases or duffle bags and disappear back into their own lives, and she would be left on her own. In this new place she would either be self-propelled or static. Her limbs chopped through the thickness like a toddler on new legs, clumsily following the deplaning passengers in rows one through twenty-two. Vi couldn't be sure if this disequilibrium would prove better. It felt different. Could different be enough?

As the overhead signage signaled her eminent arrival at Baggage Claim, a small kiosk hosting a cluttered display of postcards caught her eye. Dolphins jumped off the racks, while white sand beaches kissed gentle cerulean waters. She stopped to purchase the prettiest one before falling back into the moving mass rushing to reclaim their baggage. As the luggage began to appear on the belt, the masses dissipated into intimate clumps, each identifying and gathering the things belonging to them. Vi stood apart, searching for her suitcases. Cecilia hadn't been the only one to present her college-bound teen with the desert sand Adventurer set from Sears. Only the bright red ribbon tied around each piece signified their belonging. Cecilia's ingenious and her own impotency struck her almost simultaneously. How would she ever be able to move the two suitcases and footlocker without Cecilia? Vi's stillness seemed to attract the skycap.

"Just point them out, and I'll load them up." He flashed all of his teeth. Vi tried to reciprocate but could only push the corners of her mouth out enough to form the pout you make before you spit. "There. Ceci—My mother marked them with red ribbons."

"Your Momma must be a smart lady."

Vi never thought of Cecilia Before or After as smart or not smart. That would've been like evaluating the intelligence of her own arm or leg. Vi began to spit again in response, but nodded instead. Cecilia Before would have easily engaged this brown man in blue, but neither one of them was Cecilia Before. She followed her luggage out to the curb and into a cab in silence. The landscape sped by like one of those low budget movies where the green screen appeared too obvious because the actor in the forefront didn't quite fit into the simulated landscape. The cab zoomed under sky rise-high evergreens that she couldn't imagine feeling a part of. Did that make her the simulation? The thing to be integrated?

"This is it."

The image outside of the taxi's window reflected a memory of Chicago's infamous low-rise projects, crumbling under the weight of their names. Names like Jeffrey Manor, or Altgeld Gardens. Each one an unfulfilled promise. These buildings seemed no different. Big black letters announced Tubman Towers, though only a collection of four buildings, none of which stood more than three stories high. The small sparse courtyard featured a larger than life bronze reproduction of Harriet Tubman's body in its center. The loud clearing of the driver's throat interrupted Vi's rememory of something different yet the same. Cecilia After warned her about scratchy throats, so she handed him the few crushed dollar bills she'd stuffed into her pocket for this exact purpose, and watched as he drove away. The things she'd carried from Chicago sat unnaturally on the crumbling concrete sidewalk surrounding the wilting courtyard. Perched on the edge of the footlocker, she imagined leaving it all there. She felt hopeful for the first time in a long time.

"You need help?" A boy. Not quite a boy, but not all the way a man. "You need some help?" He repeated it louder like he thought she might have either been hard of hearing or stupid.

Is it human nature to always place the burden of understanding on the listener? "Yes." Her response as loud as his question.

He jumped.

She laughed. Another difference. It's what Cecilia told her After. That they both were different; they both had to be different.

The boy/man followed her up to the 2nd floor. 203D. The white letters spray-painted on the steel gray door from one of those templates that marked institutions; at least institutions not hiding from themselves. The doors at the Centre didn't have numbers. At the Centre they convalesced in "suites" christened with names like Magnolia and Gardenia, as if they were growing something lovely and regenerative behind each closed door. Vi pushed against the door and hoped, against her rule on hoping, the institutionalized template numbers were a lie. The door opened, releasing the dank smell of trapped air mixed with what some guy in a factory in Ohio probably thought lilies smelled like. She'd broken her rule in vain. The door's markings completely fulfilled their promise. Vi turned, but the boy/man had disappeared. When did he leave? Had she imagined him? Was he simply conjured from her need to move something she couldn't lift alone? But her trunk sat in the center of the doorway as proof of her present sanity and lack of imagination. Dr. Gabrielle's voice floated from somewhere behind her, like a warning buoy bobbing on the surface of her doubt.

— *The real and the imagined aren't the same, and you must learn to decipher the two.*

— *And if I can't?*

— *You will.*

— *But if I choose not to. Then what?*

— *Then you get to hang out with me a little longer. Is that what you wanted to hear?*

As if Dr. Gabrielle ever said anything to her she wanted to hear. Vi began to unpack her side of the room. She knew which side belonged to her because the other side was already full of Danielle, her roommate. She knew her roommate's name because it stretched across the wall in large pastel letters. Photos covered every square inch of the wall above Danielle's bed. Danielle walking the dog. Danielle at church on Sunday. Danielle with older versions of herself and younger versions of herself. Danielle asleep. Danielle awake. It seemed as if the universe had conspired to record every aspect of Danielle's life.

Even after Vi finished unpacking her things the room still looked disturbingly unbalanced, as if it would tip over from the sheer weight of Danielle's abundance and Vi's lack thereof. Where was Vi's life Before? Boys? She had been invisible. They only saw the glossy ones. The girls with glistening hair and lips that shined as if they had always already just licked them. Girls whose hips moved in chorus with hip hop mantras. She might as well have been an apparition. Girlfriends? Even though she'd spent all four years running track, none of the girls ever crossed over from teammate to confidante. Hordes of giggly gossipy girlfriends were never something she wanted. She had Cecilia, and that was enough. It had been enough. Vi dug a small photo from the bottom of her purse, the only picture she carried of her family–her complete family. The Moon crew was all there–Vi, Cecilia and her father. Vi couldn't have been more than five or six. The edges of the photo folded in on themselves, and the color began fading years ago. His face a brown blur. She couldn't remember a time when she could distinguish his nose from his lips; his cheekbones from his sideburns. She caught her reflected self in Danielle's mirror. She stood as her clearest memory of him. Her body. She would often search Cecilia for the differences between them in an attempt to find her father. Her legs were longer than Cecilia's, so she had gotten them from him, and though Cecilia could claim most of her face, Vi's deep brown, almost black eyes, stood in opposition to Cecilia's, so at the age of eight, she began to answer any inquiries about her paternity in the same way. *I have my father's eyes.* So, since then, she'd seen through his eyes. But now her eyes didn't work right. She saw things that didn't exist. That's why she'd cut herself open and ended up at the Centre. Invented a lump out of thin air. Her eyes must be bad. Did that make skewed vision her inheritance? Or would Dr. Gabrielle name it something else?

— *I have my father's eyes.*

— *Tell me about him.*

— *Why?*

—

— *My mother is my father.*

— *I'm sure she's had to do double duty, but you haven't really told me much about him.*

—

— *When was the last time you talked to him?*

— *I have no conscious memory of ever talking to him.*

— *What has your mother told you about him?*

— *That he was there and then he wasn't.*

— *Is that all? Is that enough?*

— *It was enough for me.*

— *Was?*

— *What?*

— *You said was enough. Past tense.*

—

— *Is it still enough?*

—

— *Vi?*

— *He didn't just leave me. I'm not one of those little girl's whose daddy leaves because she's black.*

— *Why would someone leave because you're black?*

— *I was watching this program on television. I'm not sure, it might have been Oprah or something just like Oprah but not, and all the people were talking about the black family crisis. Absent black fathers.*

— *But fathers of all races leave their children.*

— *But the only difference between those fathers and the fathers on T.V. is blackness, so even without saying it there's only one real conclusion.*

— *People leave people they love all of the time.*

— *Why?*

— *Love isn't always enough to keep people together. Real life is simply more complicated than that.*

— *But if two people really want to stay together?*

— *Want is not always enough.*

—

—

— *Anyway. It was different with my father. He didn't leave me with nothing. I have his sight.*

— *His sight?*

— *I mean his eyes. He gave me his eyes. That means something doesn't it?*

— *Gave? Like a gift?*

— *He didn't leave me alone with nothing.*

— *He didn't leave you alone. He left you with Cecilia.*

—

— *Vi?*

— *Anyway. I don't   I can't remember him. But I have his eyes. In a way it's better than a memory.*

—

— *Isn't it?*

— *Is it?*

The raised question mark she'd carved around her heart began to throb. Pinning the small photo to the cork over her desk, she stepped back, but the pitiful addition only magnified the vast nothing surrounding the remains of her past. Before she could take the proof of her lack down, a sudden rush of warm air spun Vi toward the door. Danielle from the pictures stood in the flesh.

"Roomie!" She cut through the thickness in the room as if protected by a force field of perkiness, throwing her arms around Vi. "I'm," she gestured toward her name on the wall as if auditioning to replace Vanna White, "Danielle. It's so good to meet you. My parents have just kept me running, and I haven't had a chance to come to campus and hang out like I've wanted to. Thank God this is their last night here. I'm putting them on a plane tomorrow back to Detroit. Good riddance, 'cause if I have to play the obedient loving daughter one more day, I think I'm going to bust. Viola right? What have you been up to? You got in today right? Who have you met? What have you seen? Any cute guys?"

"Vi."

"What?"

"I prefer to be called Vi. Hard V, long I."

"Oh. That's cute. Viola does sound kind of down homey." Danielle's mouth and eyes didn't stop moving. "Are your parents at the hotel?"

The tiny space Danielle had pried open between them with her perky exuberance snapped shut. Vi grabbed her running shoes from her bag and put them on.

Danielle looked up from snuggling one of the hundreds of pink puffs of fur littering her bed. "Going running?"

"Why do you say that?" Vi pulled the laces tighter.

"I just noticed you putting on running shoes."

"These? Just habit I guess. I do run though. Sometimes." Vi grabbed the postcard from her purse. "Right now I need to go mail this," holding up the card in an effort to substantiate her claim.

"The post office is a little hike. You want me to go with?"

"No."

The urgency of Vi's no did nothing to penetrate Danielle's force field as she jumped off of her bed, skipped to her desk, and handed Vi a folded piece of paper. "Okay. Here. Take my map."

Vi grabbed the map and sprinted out of the room, descending the steps of Tubman's Tower D two at a time. The map Danielle gave her placed the post office over the hill and to the north, but Vi didn't trust maps. At the age of eight, the world map Cecilia hung on her bedroom wall moved Egypt out of Africa. It took days to convince Cecilia Egypt was indeed in Africa. Since Cecilia hadn't accompanied Vi on her class trip to the DuSable Museum, where the truth had been revealed, the only proof she could provide were other maps. Vi had been obsessed. She finally found the proof in the most current set of encyclopedias in the school library, but her school didn't allow the encyclopedias to leave the grounds.

Exasperated, Cecilia finally acquiesced. "Why can't you let Egypt be? What difference does it make on 84th and Fairview Lane?"

She didn't answer Cecilia because she didn't know what difference it would make. She was only eight.

Vi turned north at Lincoln's Hall, and east at Booker T's Fountains. Surprisingly, the unchristened post office stood exactly where the map placed it. The even less assuming mailbox stood out in front like a sentry. She addressed the postcard but stalled on how to fill in the white space behind the palm trees and jumping dolphins. There were no palm trees and jumping dolphins in this place. Only disappearing boy/men, and wind-filled girls with people and photographic evidence of those people. She couldn't write that, could she? So instead she wrote: Dear Cecilia, I made it safely. Will call soon. Your daughter, Viola Ikwewe Moon. Vi slipped it into the mailbox, wondering why she'd written her full name and relation, as if Cecilia would have fully erased her from memory in a mere five hours. She opened the lip of the mailbox and looked in, wishing she could get the card back and write something smart or funny to show her she planned to be different in this place. But it was too late.

When Vi returned to Tubman, the only sign of the life-sized Danielle was a note pinned to her corkboard. Vi read the first few lines: STAYING AT THE HOTEL WITH MY PARENTS. SEE YOU TOMORROW. Vi exhaled, relieved she wouldn't have to spend her first night sleeping across from a girl who seemed to have bottled the wind. Her appointment with the work-study director was at 10 am. If she missed it, she might have to go back. To what? Cecilia Before was gone. There was nothing left to return to. She couldn't go back. Cecilia needed her to stay here, at school, away. She found the pill bottle in the bottom of her purse. The one Cecilia had stuffed into her hand at the airport.

After Cecilia passed her luggage to the skycap, they both stood at the curb under the close scrutiny of a tiny but unrelenting traffic officer.

"Drop-offs and Pick-ups only. Drop-offs and Pick-ups only."

Cecilia clutched the strap of her purse with both hands, as if afraid someone might snatch it from her shoulder. "I should come with you. At least to Security. It doesn't seem right to leave you on the curb."

"Why?"

"Because I'm your mother. I should see you off."

"You're seeing me off now."

"Are you sure you don't want me to come with you? I'm sure they still have seats on your flight."

"Cecilia."

"Okay. Take these." She opened her purse and peered into the bottom as if it contained and endless abyss of things she needed to give to Vi, but she only pulled out one. Vi assumed it would be more money. Cecilia had been handing her crumpled rolls of dollars for days now. Each designated for a specific purpose.

"I don't need any more money." This time instead of a roll of well-used dollar bills, Cecilia handed her a refilled prescription, identical to the filled bottle Vi purposefully left on her dresser at home.

"I had them refilled just in case. It might take you a little while to get yourself settled and transfer your prescription."

Before Vi could find the words to protest, the tiny and angry traffic officer waved her wand in their direction. "Drop-offs and pick-ups only. The tow truck will be back around in two minutes."

"Okay. Well I guess this is it. Bye Viola." Cecilia leaned in, gingerly placing her arms around Vi as if afraid an actual hug would break her. Nothing like the thick bear hugs of Cecilia Before. Nothing like them. Vi knew then leaving was the right thing to do.

Vi gripped the empty bottle tight before tossing it into the trash. She flushed the pills at the airport in Chicago, but kept the bottle. Florida would be different. Her obsessions would not follow her across state lines. She would be able to trust her eyes here. Vi lay back, closed her eyes, and willed herself to sleep.

 Giggles flowed easily from her lips into her cupped hand. The grass felt damp and warm against the bottom of Vi's feet. She ran across the backyard so fast she almost slipped.

His hand shot out to steady her. "Be careful baby."

Vi turned and grinned. She could see his big eyes shining even though it was still dark out. When the shiny part started to overflow onto his cheeks, she took his hand. "I'm okay daddy. I'm a big girl."

"Well, does a big girl need me to push her on the swings?"

Vi put one hand on her not quite a hip. "Come on Daddy. It ain't no fun if you don't push." They both raced toward the swing-set he built on her seventh birthday. Mother said it took him all night to put it together.

Maybe that's why it didn't surprise her when he woke her up while the sun slept and asked if she wanted to go play. And maybe that's why she wasn't surprised when he placed his pointing finger across his full lips in the internationally known "let's not wake mother" signal. That's why she happily jumped out of her bed, tiptoed down the stairs, and ran out the side door.

The moistness of the new morning seemed to go with the wetness smushing between her toes and the dampness on her daddy's cheeks. She sat down as her daddy held on to the bottom of the swing. He pulled her back and up until her toes dangled in front of his face. Her stomach became a C as she inhaled, waiting. Then he let her go. She tried to catch the joy in her throat, knowing they had to be quiet, that they couldn't wake mother, but it spilled out anyway. Over and over he pushed. Just when it seemed she couldn't get any higher, she saw the sun peeking over the roof of the house. She looked down to tell daddy he could stop pushing, but he wasn't behind her. As he leaned against the chain link fence, his eyes didn't leave her smiling face. Vi couldn't believe she was actually swinging so high by herself. She wanted to yell down to her daddy to make sure he saw. But she didn't have to because he was right there, watching, smiling up at her.

When he carried her back into her room and tucked her into bed, she couldn't remember ever being so happy. The next day she thought it must've been a dream, until she pulled back the covers and saw the proof stuck between her toes.

Then Mother appeared in the door of her room. Her eyes red and swollen. Her voice even when she told her.

Vi didn't believe her. Couldn't believe her.

"Daddy ain't gone. Look."

Vi waved her dirty little feet in the air. Sure that Mother could not argue with the now dry blades of grass that proved her daddy would never leave her. But Cecilia simply walked away.

Vi sat up in the bed. The unfamiliar smallness of her dorm room quickly became familiar. She couldn't remember the last time she'd remembered. Her father. This place brought him back. She remembered. Now she had more than just a faded photograph. She inhaled, feeling the hole she cut open the summer before, close a bit. Maybe the next dream would bring her closer to closing it. Maybe this place would clean the wound and heal it. Maybe. She closed her eyes, tempted to break her rule on hoping just one more time. This time, maybe, it wouldn't be in vain.

When Vi opened her eyes again, she felt more rested than she had in months. Too rested. The digital clock blinked a red 12:00 back at her. Silence echoed through the building. She grabbed her watch. 10:15. Vi snatched down the first thing in her closest and yanked it over her head, a dress Cecilia gave her. A hand me down. But Vi had been attracted to its greenness. It reminded her of spring in Chicago, mostly the spring before this summer. Vi turned away from the mirror and shook the memory from her head. This was her new beginning, and she was already late.

Vi busted into Adam Clayton Powell's Administration Center like a prom queen at a dirt bike rally. The rest of the appointees had obviously not received the memo on how to dress for success. She stood in the middle of the financial aid waiting room, a little blade of overdressed grass in a sea of t-shirts and jeans.

"Where she going? Prom?" Bodiless voices peppered the walk to the front desk. Giggles fluttered through the room as Vi made her way to the receptionist.

"I'm Viola Moon. I have a 10 o'clock appointment with Dr. Crisabel."

The receptionist looked at the clock. "You mean you *had* a 10 o'clock."

"I'm sorry I overslept. My alarm didn't go off."

The receptionist had obviously lost interest. Her head dropped back toward the document in her hand. "Have a seat."

Vi did as told. As she sat, she watched every other able-bodied, financially-lacking, alarm clock operating work-study candidate file into and out of the Work Study Director's office. When the receptionist finally motioned Vi to follow her, the clock's small hand had already passed 4 p.m. The Work Study Director, Dr. Crisabel, reminded Vi of the women she'd seen on the cover of Ebony and Jet; women who took charge of their men, their families, and their communities with frozen smiles and equally frozen hair. Vi and Cecilia Before used to make fun of those women, inventing lives full of nappy-headed chaos behind the smoothed-down edges. Photos of Dr. Crisabel standing in a group of women all dressed in silver, lined the back of her desk. Something about sisterhood adorned one of the frames. Vi attempted to mimic Dr. Crisabel's expression, hoping to encourage some sort of empathy. The glare she received over Dr. Crisabel's designer frames suggested her sisterhood didn't extend to Vi's side of the desk.

"Ms. Moon, my 10 o'clock. It's 4 p.m. Why are you just darkening my doorstep?"

"My alarm didn't go off."

"Do those things usually set themselves?"

She reminded Vi of Cecilia Before, in the way hard closed things remind you of soft open things. "No ma'am."

"Then why are you just sitting in front of me at 4 p.m."

"I didn't set my alarm." Vi placed one hand in the other and wished she could transform into one of those magical beings with wings.

"That's right Ms. Moon. Personal responsibility. You are at University now. And if you plan to stay here, then you must learn personal responsibility. Your parents have done their work. Now it's time for you to stand on your own two feet. Do you understand?"

"Yes Dr. Crisabel. I understand. I'm on my own." She knew after last summer she was on her own, but Vi had never said it out loud.

"Good. Now let's get about the business of putting you to work. Since you are the last student on my list, unfortunately the only job assignment left is in the Attic."

"The Attic?"

"The library's warehouse."

"I like the library."

"Not the library dear, the warehouse. Don't worry. You'll learn the difference soon enough." Dr. Crisabel wrote something on a form as her lips pressed together. "Take this to Dr. Locke in CAC001. He'll get you started."

At 4:15 the temperature continued to hover at the same 90 degrees she'd woken up to. Darkened circles of sweat formed in the armpits of her green dress. Vi checked the map Danielle gave her the day before. She couldn't locate any Attic or Library Warehouse, so she went to the main library and asked everyone behind a desk until she found someone who had been working there for more than four hours. The someone turned out to be a tiny woman fortified behind a desk stacked high with overstuffed manila folders.

Vi leaned over a stack of folders to get the woman's attention. "Excuse me. Do you work here?"

"Last time I checked." A sticky sweetness punctuated each word.

"I mean have you worked here for a while. I was sent over from work-study. Can you direct me to the Attic?"

"Of course dear. The Attic is right underneath you." The woman pulled a folder from the top of the stack and opened it.

"Are you sure?"

The folder closed, and the sticky sweetness fell away. "Did you ask for me to know or to guess?"

Vi stepped back. "To know."

As quickly as it fell, it returned. "Go on pass the reference section, behind the non-circulating library. There's a door marked employees only. Take those stairs down as far as they go. Knock hard on the double doors cause Locke is a little hard of hearing."

"Thank you." But Vi's gratitude fell on unhearing ears. The little woman had already receded behind her folders. Vi followed the instructions. She passed by the reference section and then the non-circulating library. Still she almost missed the door. She spotted it only because of her habit of looking for things that didn't exist. She descended two flights of stairs before reaching the bottom floor. A plaque that would've been more at home at the foot of the White House adorned one of the double steel doors. THE CRISPUS ATTUCKS COLLECTION CURATED BY DR. EURIPEDES LOCKE, PHD. Standing in front of the large doors made her feel like Dorothy, the Diana Ross version, banging on the gates of Oz. After she knocked, Vi half-expected flashing neon lights, smoke and a bedazzled Richard Pryor to emerge from the depths of the room. Instead nothing happened. After knocking for another five minutes she decided to try the knob, and the doors swung open with unexpected ease. Light bathed the cavernous room. White shelving lined with books stood along the room's perimeter. The overhead florescent bulbs reflected up from the pristine white concrete floors, creating prisms of lightness. Having nothing soft to rest against, an infinitely repeating *click-click-click* overwhelmed the space. The source, a dot matrix printer behind the only desk in the room, seemed to be printing in all corners of the warehouse. The sole inhabitant of the room didn't acknowledge her approach until she stood almost face to face with him.

He looked up without expression or surprise. "Welcome to the CAC, Miss...?" He extended his hand over the desk.

Vi extended her hand, but hesitated at the sight of the deep burgundy stains covering his fingers.

"Excuse the stains. It is an unavoidable circumstance of my employ.

Permanent marker." Red markers littered the otherwise pristine area around his desk.

"No. I'm sorry. Moon. But you can call me Vi." She forced her hand into his. Their awkward handshake confirmed the thing she already knew. There was something extraordinary about this man. There was nothing notable about his outward appearance. His hair appeared a bit unkempt, but the look could have come more from the length than lack effort. As outward appearances go, he stood out as extraordinarily ordinary, but something about the space surrounding him. It reminded Vi of those Our Lady of Guadalupe statues lining the shelves of the bodegas back home on Commercial Avenue; the ones with beams of light shooting from the Virgin Mary's pious figure. He had an aura.

"You must have done something to someone Ms. Moon to get placed up here." He didn't look at her directly. Instead he focused right above her eyes.

"Up here?"

"Up here in the Attic."

"But I had to come down two flights of stairs to get here. This isn't even the basement. It's the sub-basement."

His unfocused eyes pointed toward a large notebook laying open on his desk. "Perception is fluid Ms. Moon. Perception is fluid." He closed his book and looked in her direction, allowing an uncomfortable silence to settle between them.

Vi cleared her throat. "Mr. Locke when would you like me to start?"

"Doctor."

"Pardon me."

"It is Doc-tor Locke, Ms. Moon."

"I'm sorry. Dr. Locke."

"It is the details Ms. Moon. You will find I am a very particular man, and I enjoy the particularity of those in the employ of the University, and thus under my supervision by directive of the University."

Vi nodded.

"Your duties will be a subset of mine. Primarily I am responsible for text reclassification, moving circulating books to…" He waved his arm in reference to the hundreds of shelves already full of books. "…to non-circulating. You will primarily be responsible for the physical movement of texts from the library up to the Attic. We will, of course, work around your class schedule. Do you have it?"

"No not yet. I still have to register."

"Please drop off a copy of your registration by next week, and I will inform you of your required hours." He turned back toward the printer.

"Of course." Vi fought the urge to bow, but chose instead to back away. Dr. Locke seemed both foreign and familiar at the same time. She couldn't get out of the Attic fast enough. The basement's thin air made it difficult for her to breathe. The stairs seemed narrower on the way up than they had on the way down.

Vi returned to her dorm room to find Danielle on the wrong side of the room, staring at Vi's one photo.

"You look like your Mom. I've been waiting for you." For Danielle, waiting must've provided plenty of time to charge her force field of perkiness. Without even acknowledging her trespass into what Vi considered her personal space, Danielle began to push Vi toward the closet. "I planned to take you on a tour of campus, but it's time for dinner now. Change. I'm starving."

Vi had no strength to fight, and she had to admit she could eat. So she changed and allowed her tiny roommate to guide her back into the thickness of campus.

"Have you been to the cafeteria yet? Most of the food is a little gamey. But if you stick to the omelet station you should be okay. Blackjack makes a killer omelet, and they serve them all day."

"I don't eat eggs."

"Come again." Danielle twisted her head around as if it wasn't fully attached to her neck.

"I don't eat eggs. I never have. The first time Cecilia tried to make me eat them, I threw up all over the breakfast table. It was the first and last time eggs were served at my house."

"That's disgusting. Who's Cecilia?"

"My mother."

Danielle raised her eyebrows. "You call your mother by her first name?"

Vi nodded.

"What do you call your father?"

"I don't have a father."

"How is that possible? Who's the man in the picture above your desk? Please don't tell me I'm rooming with a real life test tube baby

"Of course not. That was my father. He's not anymore. "

"That doesn't make sense."

"I had one. Then I didn't. I don't remember much about him. I just remember being sad for a very long time.

Danielle walked without talking for a few seconds. "If someone asks, just tell them he's dead."

"But I don't know if he's dead."

"So it's not a lie. Trust me. If someone else asks, just say your father is dead." And the subject was closed, at least for Danielle. "Don't worry. No eggs, no problem. We'll find you something to eat that even Cecilia and your dead father would approve of." Danielle shrugged off the rewriting of Vi's history with the same ease she'd shrugged off Vi's nutritional limitations.

In between Danielle's intake of breath and her inevitable next word, Vi pointed toward a large crowd of students standing outside of the over-named Grand Ballroom. "What's that line for?"

"Johnny come-too-lates who were fool enough not to pre-register."

Vi stopped walking.

Danielle gazed at Vi with wide eyes. "Please tell me you pre-registered." Shaking her head, Danielle grabbed Vi by the arm and pulled her in the direction of the long line. "What would you do without me?" She ushered her through the crowd as if Vi were a petulant child.

The Grand Ballroom had been transformed into a temporary bureaucracy. Tables and bodies took up every square inch of space. Hastily hung signs marked the departments. ENGLISH, MATH, SCIENCE silently announced the classes that could be shopped. Like a woodpecker with Vi's ear serving as her resident oak tree, Danielle wouldn't or couldn't stop talking.

"Girl, I don't know why you didn't pre-register. All the good classes are closed now. You're going to be taking classes everyday at the crack of dawn. I hope you get up early. I don't start until 10 a.m. on Monday, Wednesday, and Friday, and I only have one class at 11 on Tuesday and Thursday. You really should have pre-registered."

The words spilled so incessantly from Danielle's mouth that she didn't notice Vi swing off to the right and stop at the English desk. The only class left met at 8 a.m. on MWF. She took it. Then she made her way to the Math desk. The only open Calculus class left met 8 a.m. on TR. She took that one too. Vi managed to register for a Spanish class scheduled at a reasonable time, and just had one History elective left to find.

Vi stood in front of the History desk and watched the boy sitting at the desk reading a crumpled paperback without acknowledging her presence. "Can you help me?"

He rolled his eyes to the top of his head and exhaled loudly. He placed his book open and face down onto the table.

Vi scanned the class listings on the desk. "I'd like to register for 101 at 10 on MWF."

"That's closed." He touched the cover of the book as if reassuring it of his quick return.

"How about the one at 12 p.m.?"

"Clo-sed." He touched the book again.

"How about the one at 2?"

"Cl-ose-d." Each time he responded, he added another syllable to the word closed.

Vi felt like turning and running out of the place, but knew if she started running, she'd have nowhere to stop, so instead of running she decided to do her best impression of Cecilia Before. She crossed her arms over her chest and leaned back. "Why don't you make it easier on both of us and tell me what's open."

He pointed a cotton candy pink-covered fingernail at the only class without a black thick line drawn through it. Sociology 113: HISTORICAL AND CONTEXTUAL STUDY OF THE FORMATION OF THE MODERN AFRICAN AMERICAN FAMILIAL STRUCTURES at 2 p.m. on MWF.

"I don't even know what that means."

Danielle appeared at her shoulder. "Maybe that's why you should take it. Get some real book learning. Do you smell that? It's starting to stink in here. Sign her up."

Book boy filled out her registration card and handed it back to Danielle.

"See. Done. Let's go." They turned and headed out of the ballroom. Danielle looked back over her shoulder and waved at the boy right before he returned to his paperback. "I think he was checking me out."

Vi twirled the gray blue cord around her fingers, pressed the fading seven. The phone rang on the other end, deep and shrill all at once. Vi waited and wondered where Cecilia could be. The voice that picked up sounded so very far away.

— Cecilia?

— Viola?

—

—

— I'm fine.

— You're fine?

— It's hot.

— Hot.

— Is it hot there?

— Sometimes.

—

—

— Cecilia?

— It's so quiet here now.

— Sound is everywhere here.

— Sound?

— I mean it's the opposite of quiet.

— I understand.

—

— School?

—

— Viola?

— I'm here. I got lost for a minute. I'm back. School is

— Good?

—

— Hard?

—

— Fun?

— Yes.

— All of that?

— All of that.

— You?

— Fine Cecilia.

— Dr. Gabrielle phoned. She sends her best.

— Who?

— Dr. Gabrielle sends her best. She says to call her anytime. Any

— I can't hear you. The connection must be

— Bad?

— Yes. Bad.

— Okay. Call me again.

— I will.

Vi looked at the phone, wanting to place her lips against the receiver before she placed it back on the plastic cradle. But the sighing girl behind her in the phone line had hard eyes, and Vi could feel them in the back of her head. Vi didn't need anymore holes in her head, so she hung up without a goodbye kiss. Dr. Gabrielle sends her best. Her head didn't have room for Dr. Gabrielle. Vi was better, dreaming new old memories, and the need to slice away the future had been left behind.

CHAPTER THREE

An unfamiliar sound woke her. Cecilia tiptoed to the window searching for the source of the vibrations reverberating inside of her head. The chorus grew stronger as dawn approached. Cicadas. Had it been seventeen years? Vi's 17th year. Cecilia climbed back into bed and closed her eyes. She wanted to both forget and remember, but she hadn't yet figured out how to do both. Her second chance child quietly opened Cecilia's bedroom door and climbed into bed alongside her. Cecilia could feel Vi's warm breath on her face, willing her to open her eyes, but she didn't. She needed to forget, and to open her eyes would mean being face to face with memory.

Vi shook her gently. "Cecilia, what's that noise? It woke me up."

"Cicadas." Cecilia spoke through closed eyes. "Last time they came was seventeen years ago."

Vi scooted closer to Cecilia, resting her head on Cecilia's breast the way she had done since right after her birth. It took her a minute to adjust to the right spot. "What's this?"

"What?'

"This." Vi placed Cecilia's hand on a small bump where her head had just been.

Cecilia laughed. "When you reach a certain age, new lumps appear in new places everyday."

Vi's eyebrows moved toward each other in the way that they had since right after her birth whenever she didn't like something.

"Don't worry. I have an appointment for next week." Cecilia reassuringly patted the spot next to the bump, and Vi readjusted, closing her eyes, allowing Cecilia's heart to beat for both of them.

They slept, and Cecilia dreamed what she'd attempted to forget time and time again.

A dull hum woke her up. She didn't remember falling asleep. He sat at her feet. Yes. Rubbing them. Cecilia liked the way his fist felt as it made soft gentle circles in the small of her foot. She didn't want him to stop. He looked up at her, and he knew. He was well into the ball of her left foot when the first cicada landed on his head. She'd shooed it away with a lazy wave, but the heavy-bodied insect lifted itself only to descend an inch away from its previous location. She'd shooed again. This time with more determination. The bug, now assured of her impotency, didn't even bother to flap its wings to feign escape. It simply sauntered away from her hand as if she was the unwanted pest. It stopped right at the edge of his nose, but he didn't even twitch. His hands remained on her feet, massaging both of them as if he still didn't feel or see or hear the emboldened bug.

"Your face. That thing is on your face." She wasn't sure if his inaction or her ineffectiveness pushed her growing anxiety to the surface.

"It's harmless." He concentrated on the sole of her left foot as if nothing else existed. As if the world outside of him didn't exist.

"But it...." Cecilia couldn't ignore the cicada that planted itself right at the point of his top lip and bottom lip joined.

He still didn't move. "Don't worry baby. I got you."

"I know you do, but..."

"No buts. Let me worry about that."

She picked up the magazine she'd been pretending to read and knocked the cicada off of him, but then another replaced it. She swung her magazine at that one, it flew off, and then another replaced that one. Then another and another. And in what had seemed like seconds, they both were covered with bugs. She wanted to scream, but didn't open her mouth from the fear that they would crawl into her mouth, down her throat, and cover the child she carried; her second chance child; her redemption. The lilies on the thin fabric stretched across her chest grew dark with her first mother's milk. Whiteness and light and silence covered them both. Then nothing.

Cecilia had been having slightly different versions of this dream since before Vi was born. Each time she woke up from the white silence, the cicadas had disappeared, and the man at her feet lay by her side. Those were the only bits and pieces she could recall from Vi's actual birth. Cecilia used to think it an omen. A fulfillment of a nagging belief that her child was not meant to survive, but Vi had survived. Cecilia could feel the heat emanating from Vi's skin. The cicadas' hum gave way to the cardinals' cacophony and the early street sounds, but a little time remained before either of them had to be up. Cecilia detached herself from her now soundly sleeping child and kneeled on the floor next to the bed, speaking her hopes into her clasped palms, and watching Vi's rhythmic inhalations.

CHAPTER FOUR

Vi's understanding seemed to have disappeared along with the need to slice. Three weeks into the semester and now she had trouble hearing — again. It wasn't a sudden and complete deafness like the summer before. This time it felt like someone gradually siphoning language, leaving only sounds behind, clinking and clanking against each other. She fought to match the sign to the signified; for the most part she managed; a game of concentration she had yet to perfect, but would. She had years of practice hiding her difference.

Sitting in sociology class, she struggled to translate the sounds coming from the professor into meaning. He stood at the lectern, delivering a lecture on Ghana, discussing some sort of symbol. A bird. A sankofa? At times she thought he might've been singing another language. Maybe Swahili? But the rest of the class scribbled wildly, leaving Vi wondering how they pulled meaning from the music. She searched in her bag for a microcassette recorder; to somehow record the sounds, but found nothing.

"What *boom boom* familial *boom baht* Akan?" He scanned his attendance sheet. "Ms....Moon.

Was he speaking another language? "Pardon me?

"*baht baht*, Ms. Moon. *Boom boom* families *boom baht*?

Bongos. All rhythm and bass. She didn't know if she should dance or sing.

"What do we really know about any familial structure? They're all like raindrops." The voice came from behind her. Clear and consistent. The first sign to find signification in days.

"Raindrops?" The professor's attention diverted to the voice behind her.

"Unique and different. Therefore resistant to reduction."

The professor grinned, and his bared teeth lit up his other face.

Should he have two faces? No one else in the room did. Was her sight compromised as well? Was her body beginning another shutdown?

"Okay. So to use your analogy, raindrops collectively make water, what can we say collectively about the Akan?"

"The Akan are more logical about their familial lines. Akan children belong to their mothers. Unlike here where the name follows the father."

A nodding boy twisted his head toward the voice behind her. "How is that more logical?"

"Simple. Maternity is definite, while paternity is always in question."

A girl from the corner of the lecture hall piped in. "Yeah. Haven't you seen Maury?"

The room erupted in laughter.

"Maury wouldn't be necessary if children bore their mother's names."

The nodding boy looked toward the professor for help. "But men are still physically stronger. It's survival of the fittest. Right?"

The voice from behind cut in before the professor could even open his mouth. "Actually genetic fitness is also the arena of the woman. She chooses who to procreate with which determines how strong or weak her offspring will be. She also ultimately decides to either end or not to end a pregnancy. Your survival was dependent on your momma, not your daddy."

The voice from behind rang like the St. James Cathedral bells over the din of misunderstanding.

Seemingly satisfied, the professor turned back to the board, repeating passages from a book she had yet to read, and once again signification disappeared.

Vi moved further down into her seat, hoping that her smallness would somehow translate to invisibility and deafness and muteness. She wanted to disappear from all sound; from hearing and still misunderstanding.

"What are you writing your paper on?" The hushed voice of her savior. It came from somewhere behind her. Like yesterday and the day before; like her sanity.

The one word that had consistently broken through meaningless sound rolled off her tongue.

"Diaspora?"

"Diaspora? *boom boom* What about *baht* it?"

Vi turned, struggling to match a mouth to meaning before the words faded into incoherent sound.

He leaned forward, coming into full view. He was what Cecilia Before would call girl pretty; a smooth hairless face framed with thick sparkling locs. His eyes the shape of almonds hooded with long Mr. Snuffelupagus lashes. Sometimes Vi would come across Cecilia staring wistfully out of a window or absentmindedly peering into a cup of tea, and each time Cecilia would deliver the same cryptic warning. Be careful of a man that's prettier than you. He'll bring you beautiful babies, but take half your heart.

"Poorchild."

Clarity returned. Was he another one of her constructions? A coping device is what Dr. Gabrielle had called it. Was this beautiful person real? He pushed past the retro afro attached to the beige boy sitting between them. "Tyrone you see me trying to get past you. You just gone sit there and look more stupid than you really are." He held out his left hand still whispering. "I'm Ronnie."

She grabbed onto it. It felt soft and warm and real. He was real. "Hi Ronnie. I'm Vi.

"No." He shook his head and cocked it to the side, assessing her from his seat. "You're Poorchild, but don't worry cause I'm here now. Oh shush, Dr. DotheRightThing is giving us the eye. We'll conversate after class."

When Ronnie did the talking he didn't consider it conversating because he chattered on through the rest of the class. It was wonderful. No grating of incongruent symbols against each other stood between them. Ronnie spoke, and Vi walked through his words as if they were her childhood backyard. He was her cicada, the one that returned her to consciousness and hearing, but better. It turned out Ronnie liked to gossip. By the end of class Vi knew nothing more about the family unit in 17th century Ghana, but she did know about the three-way affair going on between the two line sisters in the third row and the brother with the fade sitting in the back of the lecture hall. She knew the chubby girl two seats over with the fingernails eaten down to the white meat suffered from anorexia; and the irritatingly attentive apple polisher in the front row moonlighted as a klepto. The depth of Ronnie's seemingly unfettered access into the interior lives of others both amazed and frightened her. What would he do if he got a clear look at her unveiled? Would he pass her around with equal reckless delight? Still, at the end of class, she followed him. She didn't know his destination, but she didn't want the cacophonic music of non-language to reconsume her.

"I'm so glad I'm almost done with this paper. How about you?"

"Done? I haven't even gotten the assigned books yet." How could she read when she couldn't hear?

"But it's due next week." Ronnie grabbed her by the hand. "To the bookstore, and I'm not taking no from you." He moved all of the books from his bag to hers, and stuffed his empty bag under his shirt.

When they entered the crowded bookstore, Ronnie dropped her backpack at the front door and proceeded into the History section. Vi followed him as if watching a movie. He picked up several books from the shelves. "These are the required books for the class. Stand in front of me." He dropped all three of them into his bag and stuffed it back into his shirt. Vi watched as if in a daze, wondering why no one stopped him, including herself.

"Knowledge should be free. Fuck the Gatekeepers. Come on." Ronnie sauntered out of the bookstore appearing six months pregnant, holding his ungestated child in place. Vi shuffled behind him, grabbing her book bag as they left. She paused at the threshold, expecting some sort of siren to sound, marking her transgression, but no alarm erupted.

On the outside, engulfed by the afternoon's thick heat, Vi could barely catch her breath. She crumpled onto the first empty bench overlooking Booker T's Fountains. Ronnie continued gleefully placing the stolen texts into her bag.

Vi held her chest trying to manually control her heavy heartbeat. "Why are you so happy? That was wrong."

"Wrong? Poorchild, please. Apartheid is wrong. Jim Crow is wrong. Don't ask don't tell is wrong. That—that was your first revolutionary act."

Vi didn't feel like a revolutionary. She felt like a thief, but she attempted to raise the corners of her mouth. He sat down next to her. Quiet for the first time since she'd met him.

Vi didn't realize how much she needed him to not stop talking. "So what's your paper on?"

"Fags."

She shook her head, unsure if she'd heard right. "What?"

"You heard me. I'm writing about Ancient African fags. All these DotheRightThing Black Power Intellectuals want to pretend that homosexuality is some kind of white American sickness crap. If there were beautiful black men in Africa, there were other beautiful black men loving them. And that's what I'm writing about.

"Are you...?"

"I resist labels. I'm nothing and everything. As yet my love for God and myself have kept me from imbibing in fornication of any kind."

Vi thought she must have been hearing wrong again.

"Why are you looking at me like that? Yes. I believe in God. My God loves what he made. That doesn't mean my church isn't filled with self-hating hypocrites. What does that have to do with me? When I do fall in love, I'm not going to let a bunch of pseudo-intellectual, self-hating, closeted homosexuals decide what that person will look like."

"Is there anything you don't have figured out?"

Ronnie poked his lips out. "Have you ever been in love?"

Visions of a tub filled with bloody water, and Cecilia's scared eyes emerged. That's not the kind of love he meant. "With a boy?"

"A boy, a girl, whatever. Well, have you? You can't just leave me hanging. I've told you all my little business."

"You've told me everyone else's business. The only thing you've told me about your business is that you don't have any."

"Poorchild listens. I like. Well I promise when I get some, you'll be the first one I tell. Now spill it, or I'm going to leave you buried in this pile of diasporic confusion."

No boyfriends. No girlfriends. Just the cutting. Then the Centre and Dr. Gabrielle. She couldn't spill that. "No, not that I can remember.

"Not that you can remember? Poorchild who forgets love?"

Can't love be forgotten? "Can't anything be forgotten?" Like a father from pictures.

"You know, that may be. You could have blocked it out. In my psych class, I read about a man who couldn't remember anything before his 25th birthday."

Right. That would be like blocking out the birth of your child. Anything was possible. From the time she was six or seven, each year on her birthday Vi would ask Cecilia to recall the story of her actual birth day. Vi would wait to hear the details of where Cecilia was when her water broke, or the nervous ride to the hospital, or the hours of a labor preceding an ultimately triumphant birth, but every year Cecilia would respond the same way. Not yet. Next year. I'll tell you everything. Next year. But the next year Cecilia would give her the same answer. Eventually Vi just stopped asking. So maybe Ronnie was right. Maybe love, any love, could be forgotten. "May be."

Vi returned to Tubman's Tower weighed down by both the stolen textbooks in her backpack and her past. Safely tucked into 203D, she could only stare at the books Ronnie made her steal in the name of intellectual accessibility. Fuck the Gatekeepers he said. Fuck the Gatekeepers she repeated. Do something on patriarchy he said. But I don't have a father. Everyone has a father. Remembering Danielle and the rewriting. I mean my father is dead. Is your mother alive he asked. Of course. Well do your paper on matriarchy. He turned to a chapter in a stolen book and pointed. Matriarchy. She only stared at his finger, so he countered her inaction with action. Take these. Vi placed the two pills on top of her desk; two blue eyes taunting her. Just take one. They'll help you focus he said. The pills would help, had helped, but soon they wouldn't. Pills were temporary. The question mark around her heart began to itch. What she had couldn't be cured with pills. If her stay at the Centre taught her anything, it taught her that.

— *Viola please relax.*

— *I can't. I'm not from here.*

— *What do you mean?*

— *These things. They belong to you. I can't relax in someone else's space.*

— *Can you sit?*

— *Of course Dr. Gabrielle. I'm not a moron. What kind of last name is Gabrielle?*

— *That's actually my first name.*

— *Are you from Alabama?*

— *No. Why do you ask?*

— *I had a neighbor from Alabama and she did that?*

— *Did what?*

— *Used first names like last names. So which are you in here?*

— *Which am I?*

— *Either you're Doctor or Gabrielle.*

—

— *This room is too small for you to be both.*

— *I never thought of it that way. You choose.*

—

—

— *I choose Doctor.*

— *Okay Viola, why are you*

— *Vi. I prefer to be called Vi.*

— *Okay Vi, why are you here?*

— *I don't know. My real doctor referred me.*

— *Well. Why do you think she referred you to me?*

— *I don't know. I couldn't read her writing on the referral.*

— *What did you go in to see your doctor about the day she referred you to me?*

— *I don't remember.*

— *I really need you to try. Were you not feeling well?*

— *I found a lump.*

— *Where did you find it?*

— *Under my left breast.*

— *So you went to the doctor to see what it was?*

— *No.*

— *Why did you go?*

— *I went so she could cut them off.*

— *Cut what off? The lump.*

— *My breasts.*

—

— *You don't really need them, you know. They're just there. In the way.*

— *You want to cut off your breasts because they're in the way?*

— *Yes. You don't really need them.*

— *What about the lump? Did you have it tested?*

— *They have yet to invent a test for invisible lumps.*

—

— *That was a joke Doctor. You're supposed to laugh when someone tells a joke. It's only polite. Are you allowed to laugh?*

— *Of course I'm allowed to laugh. So is your joke a way of telling me that the lump did not exist.*

— *It existed. I'm not a moron.*

— *Of course you aren't a moron. I'm sorry if I made you feel that way.*

— *I didn't say I felt like a moron.*

—

— *You do know that you really don't need breasts?*

— *Vi why do you think we have them if we don't need them?*

—

— *Vi? Did you hear my question?*

— *Of course. I heard. I'm not a moron.*

Vi began to rub the question mark keloid through the thin cotton of her t-shirt. Dr. Gabrielle could put at least one down in the win column. She had stopped Vi from wanting to sever the things that had separated Cecilia into two parts of herself: Before and After. But did the want stop or just the words confessing to the want? The words made the need real for Dr. Gabrielle, but did they for Vi? But Vi could separate today from yesterday; the imagined from the real. Clarity had returned. Again. So she placed the pills into her desk and picked up one of the books that Ronnie stuffed into her bag and began to read. If he were there and knew her whole truth, he would probably call it her second act as a revolutionary.

"Hurry up." Danielle snatched the pillow from Vi's face.

"I'm not going." Vi wondered if Danielle experienced hearing issues too. "I have a paper due next week. I haven't even started it."

"Next week? That's a month in freshman time. All you ever do is go to class and sit up in this room. That's just unnatural. You're going. Now hurry up." Danielle disappeared from the doorway, and Vi placed the pillow back over her head. Ten minutes later Danielle reappeared, standing over her.

"I'm giving you exactly five minutes, and then I'm dragging you out of that cot."

"Danielle, I'm not—"

"Now you have four minutes and forty-five seconds. The Gamma Nus aren't going to wait all night."

"I'm not going." Vi rolled over, facing the wall.

"Their new pledge line is going to be there." She sang it, like a siren enticing a lost sailor to his death. "Juju said he'd make them do whatever I wanted them to." She added lip-gloss to her reflection in the mirror on top of the lip-gloss she was already wearing. "I mean, whatever I wanted them to."

"That sounds terrible." Vi couldn't imagine exercising control over another human being. She had enough trouble exercising control over herself.

"What's terrible? A man slave. I've been waiting all my life for one of those." She blew a kiss at her mirror image. "You have three minutes."

Vi pulled Cecilia's quilt over her head, wishing Danielle away like a bad dream.

"Juju isn't supposed to tell me, but he said the guys on this line are so weak. He said he made one of them cry over the silliest thing, and this guy is supposed to be a legacy."

Vi moved aside the worn quilted hearts. "A what?"

"You know. He's a legacy. His father was a Gamma Nu and his father was a Gamma Nu and his father was a Gamma Nu."

Vi stopped listening. A person could be a legacy? A whole body, not pieces; not lips or ears or eyes.

Danielle continued to prattle. "Cause Ju is self-made, so he has a thing about legacies. Anyway Ju is like he's not going to let anyone sneak into his frat. No matter how many Gamma Nus he has in his bloodline."

A legacy. A person could be a legacy. "Okay. I'll go."

Triumph swept across Danielle's face. "Good, cause your five minutes were up anyway."

The house looked nothing like Vi thought it would. In the movies, frat houses were antebellum mansions with manicured lawns on the outside directly opposing the debauchery spilling from the inside. This small white frame bungalow couldn't have held more than three, four bedrooms tops. Kids milled about outside like any house party. Vi exhaled. This she could do.

Danielle must have felt the tenseness dissipate. She turned toward Vi. "See it's not so scary, is it?"

Vi decided any affirmation would be premature before stepping inside. Crimson bulbs glowed throughout what would've been the living room and dining room if there had been furniture left in the rooms to define them. Gyrating bodies filled both rooms. The music and bodies moved together with each vibrating pulse emanating from the speakers. The tall thin-faced boy Danielle referred to as Juju popped out of the crowd and pulled Danielle's pseudo-resisting frame into the melee.

Vi stood apart in the crammed room; unsure of how to proceed. Despite the open windows, hot air hovered undisturbed. Vi wiped her palm against her forehead.

A girl with a yellow plastic cup covered in condensation waved it at her. "There's punch in the kitchen."

Vi moved toward the punch. Most of the boys crowded into the small kitchen were together. Vi knew they were together because they wore identical black jumpsuits and combat boots. They stood in a semicircle around the table with the punch. One of the boys stood directly behind the bowl with a ladle held in mid-air in one hand and a plastic yellow cup in the other. His eyes held steady on the liquid in the bowl.

"Can I have a drink please?"

Each jump-suited figure began to echo her request in a deep resonating cadence while surrounding her. It sounded like the call began in the depths of hell. Vi could see the smiling faces of others outside of the circle, but they couldn't drown out the stern faces of the boys standing as a living prison around her. Vi willed herself not to run. It was college. Fraternities were steeped in history. Fraternities were steeped in secret ritual. As the chant ended, the boys all dropped their jumpsuits to their ankles in a staccato-syncopated rhythm, revealing various incarnations of cartoon-emblazoned underwear. The room exploded in laughter, and Vi realized fraternities were also steeped in humiliation. The boy with the cup and ladle filled it and handed it to her without ever establishing eye contact. The circle opened and the boys returned to their original formation. Vi's hand shook as she accepted it, but the overly-sweet purple liquid went down easy. Her pounding heart was no longer in competition with the bass throbbing from the speakers in the living room. Before she could exhale, all of the jump-suited flashers ran out of the kitchen just as Danielle ran in.

"Girl I've been looking for you everywhere. The slugs are up. Juju says this is going to be the best part." Danielle's eyes rested on the empty yellow cup in Vi's hand. "Shit you haven't been in that blue juice have you. They told us all about it at orientation. How many cups did you have?"

Vi held up one no longer shaking finger.

"You should be okay. Just stay close." Danielle dragged Vi through the now empty house and out the front door, elbowing and pushing her way through the pulsating crowd forming a circle on the front lawn. The jump-suited flashers stood in line at the center of the circle with each boy's ankle shackled to the boy in front and behind. Danielle's Juju stood outside of the line chanting undecipherable instructions to the boys, and the line began to dance in unison. But Vi felt one of the pledges before she could clearly see him. He stood in the middle of the line; almost indistinguishable from the other shaved heads in dark jumpsuits. Something about his cadence; his repetition of the well-practiced steps; the perfectly calculated lift of his shackled leg that resonated familiar; even though he almost kept perfect rhythm with his line brothers his apartness seemed obvious, at least to her. Vi had seen fake chains before, and these weren't. Pink raw skin began to appear in the exposed window of flesh between the pledge's boot and jumpsuit. A wince climbed up from his ankle, clambered across his chest, and settled into his bottom lip as the shackle continued to travel up and down his bare leg, leaving more of him exposed with each movement. Just as the shackle, now biting into his shin, began to draw blood, he faltered. Without thinking, Vi bent down and took up the slack on the chain connecting him to his line brothers. His eyes never left the back of the shaved head in front of him, but the circle of spectators inhaled at once as one unit. She couldn't be sure if the sudden lack of oxygen or the redistributed weight of the chains contributed, but his falter exploded into something more, something all-inclusive. She dropped the chain, but it was too late. He fell and when he did, each one of the chained boys followed him to the ground. Danielle took a step back. Vi couldn't read the look on her face, but it replicated all of the faces surrounding her. Vi stood alone.

Danielle's Juju parted from the clump and walked up to the boy who Vi attempted to help. "Are you kidding me? You think you gone sneak into my frat on some bloodlines. Your father carried it, and his father carried it, and his father carried it, but that don't mean you will."

Vi had known without knowing this boy was the legacy, a part of many.

Other members of the fraternity in various physical interpretations of Juju separated from the crowd and pushed her away from the line. They began to scream into the ears of the fallen boys. A weak link breaks the chain. A weak link breaks the chain. A weak link breaks the chain. It all began to converge in her stomach and climb back up the way it went down. She heaved once and blue juice spewed at Juju's feet.

"Danielle get this drunk bitch out of here. She almost threw up on my Jordans."

Danielle shot a look at Juju as if to rebuke him for his language. Her lips even parted, but no sound came out. Instead she turned toward Vi. "Come on." Danielle hesitated before grabbing Vi's hand and leading her away from both the crowd and the house. After a few minutes of walking in silence, Danielle sat down on a curb. "Why'd you do that?"

"I don't know what was in that stuff, and the heat and the people. I told you I didn't want to go. It was all too much for me. Before I knew it, it was coming up as fast as it went down."

"Not the throwing up part. Why did you grab the chain?"

Vi didn't have an answer. How could she explain about the boy? About how they were both pieces?

"What's wrong with you?" Danielle stared at Vi as if seeing her for the first time. "You can't interfere with the line. Who does that? Who breaks the chain?"

"But the chain didn't break."

"It's a metaphor Vi." She rolled her eyes to the top of head. "Is this your first time around black people?"

Vi didn't know how to answer the question. Wasn't she black people?

"Do you not know how serious this is? We take our Greeks serious."

"I've seen it on television and—"

"No that's white greeks."

"Are there any other kind?"

"Are you this ignorant? Black Greeks. Alpha Phi Alpha. Delta Sigma Theta. Gamma Nu. Black fraternities and sororities don't play that shit. You never never interfere with a line."

Vi's impotence stood on her shoulders. She tried to shrug out from under the weight, but Danielle misread the gesture for apathy.

"I give up. I'm trying to teach you about yourself. I'm trying to teach you how to be here. This is a historically black university."

"I told you I didn't want to come, but you wouldn't hear me."

Danielle threw up her hands and walked away.

She had seen that before. Dr. Gabrielle. Exasperating. Dr. Gabrielle would say. She felt like she won when she saw Dr. Gabrielle's back before the end of their sessions. Now watching Danielle's narrow back move away from the curb, Vi followed her back to Tubman, feeling lost.

Back in the room, Vi couldn't sleep. She couldn't stop thinking of the boy with the forefathers. She couldn't stop seeing the skin under the skin that had been rubbed away by the chain around his ankle. She couldn't stop remembering the look in his eyes when she lifted the chain. By the time her eyes closed, the sun had begun peeking out over the evergreens at the edge of campus.

When the light streaming through the window woke her, Vi felt like she just closed her eyes. Danielle lay on her bed, mouth wide open still in the comfortable confines of a deep sleep. Vi felt more awake than she could ever remember being. When she moved to go to the bathroom, she noticed it. A small child, a baby really, lying next to her on the narrow bed. The child's fat brown arms and legs swung at the air, so Vi picked her up and placed her to her breast as if she'd done it hundreds of time before. The suckling child's limbs relaxed as she latched on and milk began to flow. But almost as soon as the child began to relax, the milk began to seep from the corners of her mouth. Vi attempted to remove her breast from the baby's mouth, but the baby just began to pull harder. Light streams spilling from the baby's mouth grew stronger and faster. Gurgling noises emanated from her tiny nose. Vi remembered reading something about babies being able to drown in a teaspoon of water and began to panic. She wedged her index finger between the baby's gum and her breast, and the child, angry at the interruption, bit down on Vi's finger, but it was too late. The bond was broken. The child stared up at Vi with Cecilia's eyes before releasing an agonizing scream. Vi closed her eyes to block out both the child's accusing eyes and hunger. Then silence. She opened her eyes and the baby was gone, along with all signs of the disastrous feeding. Vi lay still, running her hands across her now aching breasts, knowing this was more memory than dream. She lay still until the beeping alarm clock woke her roommate. Danielle woke, barely casting a glance toward Vi or her side of the room. Her anger from the night before still too fresh. Vi never thought she would miss the sound of Danielle's continuous chattering, but she did. Especially now that the incident at the frat house had been crowded out by this hungry baby with Cecilia's eyes.

Too caught up with the dream to think for herself, for the rest of the morning, Vi followed Danielle. When Danielle brushed her teeth, Vi brushed her teeth. When Danielle grabbed her backpack, Vi packed her backpack. When Danielle left Tubman's Tower to go to breakfast, Vi walked behind her, keeping pace with the *pit pat* Danielle's flip-flops made against her smooth heels. But the *pit-pat pit-pat* only moved the child and the sound of her persistent feeding to the center, until the whispers and not-so-whispering denunciations of the people they passed pushed the baby toward the edge. She'd been outed. She might not have been the first to throw up at the frat house this semester, but she was the first to interfere with the line. She would now and forever be the breaker of the chain. Vi arrived in the dining hall to looks of both amusement and disgust. In the crush of her judge and jury classmates, she lost sight of Danielle. Without guidance, Vi found herself in the least populated space in the food line, face to face with Blackjack and the omelet station.

"What you need?" Blackjack was half white. Not in the sense of racially-diverse parentage, but diverse genes, vitiligo. He stood behind the omelet station a living sign of America's melting pot, the white side of him melting over his blackness, erasing it a little at a time. First an eye, then a nose. His black mouth, still untouched, and tired of waiting, opened again. "What you want in your omelet sweetheart?"

She wanted to sleep without dreams. She wanted Cecilia Before. She wanted to not be different. She wanted to belong to this place and these people. "Everything."

He moved the spatulas like Picasso's brushes. Stirring and caressing the gelatinous mess into something uniform and stagnant before placing it on Vi's plate and sending her on her way. Without Danielle's bob in front of her, Vi chose her own space in the dining room. With Danielle, the transition to this place had at least been thoughtless. Danielle in front. Always leading her. From day one, Vi followed Danielle across campus, to the dining hall, through the food line, into the dining room and to a perfectly situated table which Danielle instantly christened "their" table. Now alone, Vi felt like a refugee. Danielle now sat at "their" table, but the rigid straightness of her back clearly communicated Vi's expulsion, so Vi moved through the sparsely populated dining room until she reached an unoccupied corner. With her back to the rest of the cafeteria, she began to eat the omelet. The first bite surprised her. It was the best thing she'd ever tasted, signaling one more aspect of herself that she was a complete stranger to. As she shoveled the three egg omelet, loaded with everything from Blackjack's prep station, into her mouth, she imagined all of the opportunities she'd missed, with quiche, eggs benedict, eggs sunny side up. Her hunger surprised her, and the emptying plate on the table was neither sign nor signification of her satisfaction. She wanted another one, but before she could get up and make her way back through the line, the memory of the violent unsatiated suckling rang in her ears. The cloying scent of spoiled milk coupled with her previously upset stomach. Her hand was too slow and too singular to stymie the resolute and immediate betrayal of her digestive tract as Blackjack's work of art returned to its gelatinous roots becoming, ironically, really akin to Picasso's pieces as it splattered across the table. Vi sat covered in what she always knew she wouldn't be able to swallow, unable to decipher—the caustic sounds traveling through the dining hall. A familiar hand squeezed her shoulder, while its well-manicured partner wiped her face from behind.

"If this is going to become a habit, you're going to have to buy me some rubber gloves."

Vi could only manage to push her lips in the direction of a smile, as Danielle pulled her up from her chair and guided her to the bathroom and away from the cacophony of the dining hall's non-language.

CHAPTER FIVE

Cecilia woke up. A late morning sun followed her soft footsteps into the nursery. Stillness hanging over the crib didn't alarm her. She reached for the child the way she had a hundred times before, and the baby found the fullness of her breast with ease, sighing with satisfaction. Cecilia's milk came down quickly. But even after the baby's small abdomen began to tighten from fullness, the baby sucked. She continued sucking even after Cecilia's warm milk backed up into her tiny throat and seep out of her puckered lips. Cecilia feared she would have to yank the baby's head from her neck to break the bond between them. The soft rivulets of milk streaming down the sides of the baby's cheeks grew stronger, eventually forming puddles on the floor, but the baby only sucked harder. Milk spewed out of the child's mouth and nose, finally forcing the child from Cecilia's breast and her arms. The loud smacking of the baby's lips echoed through the room even after she disappeared under the translucent liquid. Cecilia waited for panic to rise up from her belly as she lost sight of the child, but it didn't. When she finally spotted the lifeless form bobbing peacefully on the surface, Cecilia thought even like that, she was beautiful, like a pretty baby doll. Perfect. Cecilia heard something escape her lips, but the voice didn't belong to her, and this dead drowned child didn't belong to her. A familiar voice called out again, and Cecilia was able to place it. Vi, her second chance. The one who stopped this nightmare stood on the other side of this, waiting, and Cecilia only needed to open her real eyes to see her.

Cecilia opened her eyes to a pale gray room. Bubbling paint erupted from the ceiling where water had memorialized its path of infiltration across the outer edge and down the wall.

Her hovering daughter called out. "Cecilia. Cecilia."

Cecilia could hear tears in Vi's voice. She twitched her nose first, watching through barely open eyes as her child's breath stopped for a moment. "Smells like death in here." Cecilia peeked through one eye.

"Stop playing dead. That's not funny and you aren't dying." Vi couldn't hide the panic in her eyes.

Cecilia extended her hand as an olive branch.

Vi hesitated but took it.

"Who said me? I'm talking about her?" Cecilia nodded toward her roommate on the other side of the gray curtain.

The woman had been dying for days, at least it's what she announced at least ten times a day. If her resolve to live were half as strong as her resolve to die, she would've been cured.

Cecilia squeezed Vi's hand. "Biopsy back?"

Vi focused on the clouded windowpane and didn't squeeze back.

Cecilia understood. The returned dream was a confirmation. She didn't need to see the report. Her breasts were poison. They would have to be removed. "I'm going to tell him that he can take them?"

Vi abandoned the window and focused on Cecilia. "Then what will be left?"

"All of me." But Cecilia couldn't erase the drowned dream child from her thoughts. She struggled to keep defeat out of her voice.

Vi shook her head like she used to at the age of three. "No."

"The rest of me. The best parts of me."

"Won't you miss them?"

"Miss them. Of course not. You. I would miss you."

Vi shook her head in disagreement. "You're not going to die. Maybe we should get a second opinion."

"No. I don't need them."

"Why do you have them if you don't need them?" She released Cecilia's hand.

"Maybe if I were younger. Maybe if your father were…. No. They're of no real use to anyone anymore." Cecilia laughed, but her laughter hung in the air unreturned.

"How are you supposed to feed your babies?"

This time Cecilia shook with laughter. "Babies? Vi, you are my only baby. And you're a sixteen-year old almost woman. You can feed yourself." Cecilia hoped without them the drowning dream child would go away for good this time. Her child, her real child, stood here in front of her. The one in her dreams was a warning that her breasts would mean the end of both of them. "You're big enough to feed yourself."

Vi's exterior began to crumble. Tears crept down her face. "I'm sorry. You're right. We don't need them." She crawled into the Cecilia's small hospital bed and laid her head on Cecilia's chest carefully to avoid the place where they cut away only the first of much more.

Cecilia ignored the pain emanating from Vi's careful contact with her bandage. She took her child into her arms and pushed the dream child out of her mind. Removing her breasts was the only choice.

CHAPTER SIX

Danielle changed after Vi broke the G-Nu chain. What had once blown like a tempest, now trickled like a draft. Danielle bottled everything around Vi, with, of course, a few exceptions: Danielle gushing during a late afternoon phone call with Ju; Danielle huddled conspiratorially with one of the dozens of girls that would somehow only drop by when Vi should've been in class; but each release vanished quickly at first sight of Vi. Danielle, of course, still offered banal critiques of the local weather or rhetorically inquired about a class, but the gusts of inappropriate prying into Vi's nonexistent private life were history. When Danielle met Vi's query about the boy in the chains with a blank stare, Vi categorized their brief past as virtually unrecoverable.

"Who? The legacy? Don't waste your worry on him. He's fine. His father will make sure of that."

Lucky for Vi, even with Danielle's irrevocable difference, Vi still had the hungry baby as company. Every night the baby visited, and each morning Vi would wake with such trepidation even Danielle's silent apathy began to feel like comfort. Still, her first day of work-study couldn't arrive soon enough. A distraction she needed to keep both feet in place. This mysterious baby wanted to take her back to a place that didn't exist— but work, the Attic—did exist. Who would've thought she would actually end up looking forward to descending into Dr. Locke's subterranean lair.

When she reentered CAC, it seemed larger and sparser than the time before. But Dr. Locke however, remained unchanged; still crouched in the same position at the same desk since the day of their introduction. The constant clickety-click of the printer serving as a metronome, marking time. It seemed as if he had simply signed out of the required back and forth involved in the universal daily routine; no microwaved leftover spaghetti and meatballs or hurried tepid shower from pipes with no water pressure; no bed illuminated by the light of Letterman's monologue broadcasting from an unwatched television. Protected by the steel wartime ship he called a desk and fortified by the printer's consistency, Dr. Locke appeared to have slashed right across the edges of life's monotony, choosing instead to stick to the center; his Center.

Dr. Locke looked in her direction without meeting her eyes. "Ms. Moon. Welcome back to the Attic. I hope you are ready to work." He snapped closed a pebbled black ledger. "It seems the Administration's need to remove seminal texts from popular circulation has grown exponentially this semester. Do you have any experience with the Library of Congress?"

"I've been in libraries my whole life." For Vi, the library had always been her respite, even as a small child. When most children would bounce with glee at the news of an impending visit to the zoo or toy store, Vi became almost unbearable once told a visit to the library was scheduled. Her favorite was story time. The children's librarian, Mr. Sam, a wide-chested grizzly bear of a man with a pliable voice that easily lent itself to hero and villain alike. She would often request *The Giving Tree*. Even though she'd heard it time and time again, each time she would hold her breath in anticipation of the tree making a different decision. Each time her little heart wished for the tree to finally say no to the selfish boy, but no matter how much she wished, the tree continued to sacrifice itself over and over.

"This is not the Dewey Decimal System of your local public library Ms. Moon. This is a University. The Library of Congress is vastly different."

Vi knew it all ultimately culminated in a collection of letters and numbers, and since she'd been reading since the age of three, she doubted it would be a problem. His eyes shifted to meet hers. "I'm sure I can figure it out Dr. Locke."

"Ms. Johnson, please show Ms. Moon what she needs to know."

A girl appeared. Vi assumed the girl must've always been there, but she'd just been too focused on Dr. Locke to notice. Vi waited for further instruction, but Dr. Locke returned to muttering to himself as he reopened the giant ledger and checked the pages spewing from the antiquated printer. He handed a stack of papers to Ms. Johnson without looking up, and Ms. Johnson nodded in the direction of an empty pushcart, so Vi followed her out of the warehouse and into the service elevator. Once in the elevator, the girl handed Vi a map of the library.

Vi waited for the girl to show some recognition of either her digestive betrayal or breaking of the chain, but she didn't. Maybe the whole campus didn't share one brain. "Thanks Ms. Johnson."

"Stop tripping. My name is Tunisia. Yours?" Tunisia had a way of pausing before she spoke, as if reading from a script.

"Vi."

"Well Vi, this is a pretty sweet gig for the most part. I was working upstairs last week, but they decided since I worked down here last year they would send me back to help out with all these new pulls. Dr. Locke is a strange dude, but he pretty much leaves you alone if you don't ask too many questions. He hates questions. You from Chicago?" She turned toward Vi with an exaggerated flourish.

Vi looked around for a hidden audience. She saw no one and wondered who this girl was performing for. "How'd you know?"

She gave Vi another side-glance that would have been more at home on a Broadway stage than the Attic. "I figured you was from somewhere up North. I was gone say Detroit next."

Vi followed Tunisia's practiced steps onto the freight elevator, then the fourth floor, as Tunisia continued her assessment.

"I'm from all the way down south, Hotlanta." She pointed toward the number four next to the elevator. "I like to start at the top and work my way down." Tunisia pulled out the print-out. "Looks like we're headed to World History first. We pull books in two categories: temp and perm. Temp go to the attic, and the perm go to the incinerator."

Tubes of fluorescent light flickered in History. Vi found the constant on and off disconcerting. Its unevenness reminded her of a place she'd been but didn't want to return to. "We destroy books?"

"We don't. The engineers do. We just mark them as permanent pulls."

The books on most of the shelves looked as if they'd been undisturbed for years, yet the thought of their ultimate destruction saddened Vi. She ran her hand across each book's spine as she passed. E. Moon. She stopped and pulled it off of the shelf. E. Moon. Her father was E. Moon. She remembered the envelope. It was the prettiest shade of robin's egg blue. Easily distinguished from the white envelopes and brightly colored sales circulars. E moon scribbled in the top corner. Of course there had been more between the E and the Moon, but it looked like indistinguishable scribble to her prepubescent eyes. Funny how things were triggered. How memories pushed through like the tips of tulips every spring, but not always as pretty or perfectly formed. Cecilia had taken the envelope and disappeared into her robin's egg blue bedroom. It was the last time Vi had seen the envelope. Vi placed the book on the cart.

Tunisia turned as if stung. "That ain't on the list."

"What?"

"Nothing goes on this cart without it being on the list. Locke will lose it." She placed her hands on her hips, and eyed Vi suspiciously.

"I'm not pulling it for storage. It's for me."

"Maybe you need to get your own cart. Cause don't nothing go on my cart that's not on the list."

Vi removed her recovered memory from the cart and turned to return to the Attic for her own cart when a low grunting interrupted her.

Tunisia's bad attitude immediately dissipated as she placed a finger to her lips and motioned for Vi to follow her.

Vi put the book back on the cart and trailed behind her. "Where are we going?" Tunisia didn't respond, so Vi continued to follow her. The grunts grew louder, interrupting the South Pacific's silence. The hot air smelled of sweat and funk.

Tunisia pointed to shadows feeding on themselves in the corner.

"Are they?"

Tunisia nodded. "I come up here and watch sometimes. You'll be surprised what people do when they think nobody watching. It's some nasty ass girls up on this campus, and you can't never tell how nasty they are by looking at them."

There were no faces, only dark outlines pushing against each other.

Tunisia slammed the *Anthropological Genetics in Melanesia* onto the floor, and the pushing shadows froze. "Smell like ass and fritos up in here. This library need to invest in some air freshener." The sultry shadows parted, and a hard laugh fueled with self-righteousness rose from Tunisia.

Vi felt like throwing-up.

Tunisia didn't notice her discomfort. She reentered her one-woman show behind the cart undeterred. "You got someone special?"

Vi couldn't get the pushing shadows or Tunisia's mean laughter out of her head. Those shadows looked like they were feasting on each other. "No." A sudden cramp nearly bent her over.

Tunisia didn't acknowledge Vi's pain or divert from her script. "Well if you ever get somebody, don't bring him up in here. Unless you want the whole campus to know your business."

The whole campus? Were the two of them enough to make the whole? Vi recovered E. Moon from Tunisia's cart for the second time. "How about you give me the other half of the list? I think I got it." She needed to get away from this girl, the shadows, and the sticky scent of unsanctioned sex.

Tunisia clutched the sheets to her chest in the first non-deliberate action she'd demonstrated since they'd met. Recovering quickly, she handed Vi more than half of the print out. "Suit yourself, but you still gone have to go back up to the Attic to get your own cart."

Luckily, Vi found an abandoned cart in the Fijis. By the close of her shift, she made it halfway through the remains of the 2nd floor Archaeology section when he appeared like a lost relic; like discovering a perfectly preserved Woolly mammoth in the mountains of Montana. The boy in chains, the one with too many fathers to count, sat alone at an isolated study table. Vi moved closer. He didn't notice. He sat in solitude, writing as if his life depended on recording every word the moment it encountered his consciousness. Vi stepped closer, unintentionally knocking her pushcart into a bookshelf. *Cambridge's Archaeology of South Africa* toppled from the edge of one of the shelves, and the boy's shoulders stiffened, and Vi stood still. He gathered his pad and pencil without looking back to trace the cause of the disturbance. She wanted to ask him about his leg and line, but he already had his backpack slung across his shoulder. Vi opened her mouth, but before she could call out to the boy in chains, a familiar breeze wrapped itself around her, blocking the space between them.

"Poorchild." Ronnie moved toward her at the speed of light "Poorchild, I've been crawling through this museum of dead ideas for a half an hour looking for you. Heard you went all in at the G-Nus'. Who knew I created such a monster. You ain't playing with this revolutionary stuff. I wish I was witness to the toppling of all of those misogynistic Neanderthals."

"It wasn't like that. It was …" Her eyes found the spot the boy occupied, but he had disappeared. The boy with the chains was gone—gone like Cecilia Before—but in his place he left no After, only emptiness.

By the time she returned to Tubman, Vi felt mentally exhausted. She headed straight for the phone, pressed the familiar numbers, and listened to the now familiar voice of Cecilia After. At one time Vi couldn't have imagined anything about Cecilia After ever being familiar.

— I had a   a dream the other night.

—

—Cecilia?

— Yes?

—

—Was it a sweet one? You should always share the sweet ones. Vi?

—Yes?

—Tell me about it.

—   I dreamed about Daddy. On my birthday. He gave me a swingset.

—He did?   He did. I remember.

— What happened   to it?

—We moved. We couldn't take it with us.

—Oh.   I remember.

—   Dr. Gabrielle called again. She said she still hadn't heard from you.

—

—   Will you call Dr. Gabrielle?

— Yes.

— Promise.

— I promise.

Vi placed the phone into its cradle and returned to her room. Cecilia After only wanted to hear the good dreams. She had no room in her After for drowning babies, even if they did belong to her. Vi had been looking forward to Danielle's silent presence to drown the silences between her and her mother, but all of Danielle's peppering of the other side of 203D was gone. It surprised Vi, but shouldn't have. She didn't blame Danielle for leaving. The question mark around her heart began to throb. After all, who wanted to room with a crazy girl. She had been institutionalized. She'd also broken the chain and decorated the dining hall with Blackjack's Picasso. And then of course, there was the dream baby. She thought her time at the Centre had cured her. But there was no cure. Dr. Gabrielle knew that, even if she would never admit it.

—*Dr. Gabrielle, don't you ever get tired of this?*

—*Of what?*

—*This. The questions. The answers. Don't they run into an ocean of sameness?*

—*Honestly? Everyone has a unique story even if the facts are identical. Each person's truth is different.*

—*Same facts, different truth?*

—*It's my job to help them find their truth. So when it starts running into an ocean of sameness, I'll have stopped doing my job.*

—*Cecilia and I share our truth, or we did Before.*

—*But you are two separate people. How do you think that's possible?*

—*She's my mother. My blood.*

—*What about your father?*

—*What about him?*

—*Why don't you share that same connection with your father? Don't you share his blood?*

—*I shared more than Cecilia's blood. We shared the same body. Her heart beat for me. My father didn't do that.*

—*Do you mean your father couldn't do that?*

Couldn't or wouldn't didn't matter. He didn't. He didn't, and now he was almost unrecoverable; bits and pieces collected from a broken consciousness. Would Ronnie's pills help? To take them meant she was sick. That the dream could only be a dream. The child—a construction of a broken mind—something to be forgotten, cured. Her hand rested on the book on her desk. The one she found in the library. She didn't check it out because she had no plans to return it. E. Moon. Enough had been forgotten. Vi laid down on her bed, cradling E. Moon. Elaine Moon. Not her father. Of course not. *Untold Tales*. These were Elaine Moon's *Untold Tales*, not E. Moon's. But weren't they all the same? She opened the book and began to read. It was midnight by the time she finished. She had a paper due Wednesday. She would have to pretend to not be crazy later. She still had Ronnie's pills, but she wasn't going to take them, or write about Ronnie's stolen matriarchy. She would write about Elaine Moon and her untold stories; her oral histories. She knew this woman was not her father, but tonight she was the closest thing she had to him. The clocked flickered 3: 30 by the time she finished writing, and she collapsed into a sleep absent dreams.

Vi received the paper back and imagined the F on the top stood for her Freedom.

Ronnie appeared at her side, waving his B, which she knew without reading, stood for Bullshit. "What you get Poorchild?"

She handed him her paper.

"Fuck."

"No Freedom."

"Freedom will soon mean free to work for food." Ronnie began reading. A stream of warm air escaped from his pursed lips. "You are on some real shit right here Poorchild. Ahead of your time." He read the remarks on the bottom. "He's going to give you a chance to revise it. Leave it to me. I'll dumb it down for Dr. Dotherightthing."

Vi couldn't understand. He had brought her back to clarity. Why did this beautiful strong boy keep helping her? She couldn't think of any way to find out save asking him. So she did. "Why?"

It seemed as if Ronnie had finally been asked a question that he did not have an answer to.

"Why do you care if I fail or not? Why do you help me?"

"Poorchild, I am you. And we have to help ourselves don't we. There are no knights in shining armor coming for either of us." He playfully pushed his shoulder against hers. "He's giving you until Monday to revise. I'll have it for you by Saturday."

Vi stepped into the Attic. She didn't have to look at the clock to know it was at least thirty minutes past her assigned start time. She'd overslept. The baby/nightmare made sleep impossible. This thing was too persistent to be imagined. Had Cecilia had a child before Vi? Who had come between them even before she was born? Whoever she was, she wasn't going away easily–but neither had her last illusion.

 —*Vi where were you when you felt the lumps?*
 — *In bed. With Cecilia*
 —
 —*I put my head on her shoulder*
 —*No Vi. Not Cecilia's lump. Yours.*
 —*What?*
 —*When did you fist discover the lump in your breasts?*
 —
 —*Vi do you remember?*
 —
 —*Vi?*
 —*No. I guess it was always there or*
 —*Or?*
 —*or never.*

Dr. Locke sat where he always sat, behind his desk pushing his marker across a formerly unmarked control sheet. His immutability was beginning to not surprise her. The printer played background rhythm to her approach. As she approached his desk, he dropped the marker and looked directly at her.

"Ms. Moon. Glad you could join us this afternoon." *click click clack.*

She took the list from his hand unsure if she should apologize, or get to work. As she began to move toward an empty cart, he spoke.

"You don't like it here Ms. Moon?" *click click clack click click.*

"Of course I do. I enjoy working here."

"What do you enjoy most regarding your employ?" *click click clack click.*

"The solitude is nice."

clack click click. "The solitude? But you are surrounded Ms. Moon." He pulled the sheets from the printer. "These underappreciated manuscripts of our collective past sit in direct opposition to any claim of solitude." He absent-mindedly brushed his palm across his damp forehead, but his focus remained on the white sheet of paper he pulled from the printer. A wide red smudge followed his hand. "This is reprehensible. How could they? This must be a mistake." Locke picked up a phone Vi hadn't noticed before. Had it always been there? "Dr. Shamus, this is Dr. Locke from the Attic. I need to talk to you. I just received a report that cannot be right. *The Dhuoda of Septimania's Liber Manualis* is going into permanent storage. *clack click click.* How is that possible? *click click clack click click.* Dhouda's handbook for William? *click click* Of course I have continued to edit the pull list. *click clack click click* I understand, but these bean counters don't understand the importance of each of these voices. Can you define culture? What would we be if we only valued the popular? *clack click.* Dr. Shamus please let the record show that this is under extreme protest, and the educational pursuits of our student body will surely be hindered by this blatant censorship. *click click clack.* Good Day Dr. Shamus." Dr. Locke placed a large red asterisk next to *The Dhuoda of Septimania's Liber Manualis* and handed it to Vi. "Forgive them for they know not what they do. Ms. Moon. Be sure to bring this book directly to me. Do you understand?"

She nodded, and he returned to scanning and slashing as if she disappeared alongside his need for her. The rhythmic clatter of the printer continued to provide an external heartbeat to his protestations.

Vi pushed the cart into the elevator and pushed the up arrow. Despite his eccentricities, Vi admired Locke. There was something in his essence she wanted to copy. He seemed at ease. Certainly not with all things external; the external world seemed as foreign to him as this place felt to her, but his ease with his singularity. Was that it? He stood alone, but he wrapped solitude around himself like bulletproof glass. She pulled his book first, placing it in the corner of the cart. She was alone here too, but she also had a mother that had been sliced in two. Any bloodline so easily disjointed by a surgeon's scalpel had to be questioned. Is that who the dream baby was? The question. The wheels of the cart stopped suddenly. Something had wrapped itself around the wheel well, stymieing the rotation. She moved to untangle the front wheel and bumped into a chair someone had failed to push back beneath the desk. Still exhausted from a restless sleep, she sat down. She spotted it, just as her eyes began to close. Another E. Moon. This one was Brenda first. Brenda E. Moon. *The Mycenean Civilization.* Vi rested her head on her hand as she read Brenda E. Moon's take on the Myceneans. In the dark cool recesses of the Classics, she read of a civilization long past and drifted off.

Her father was God-like, faceless, completely capable of making a world in eight, if not seven days. His hands felt rough as he marked her face with the symbol of their line. The Lamb. She stood in place naked above his people, their people, multitudinous as the desert sand. Her kinswomen came first, gently painting her naked body. The red clay felt cold against her exposed skin. She stood at the mouth of the ravenous volcano, her kinsmen a brown wall behind her. Her father, a distant God in crimson and gold robes, below. It waited for her. Her sacrifice would mean the survival of a people. The crops would be plentiful, fertilized by her spilled blood. Only through her body would they survive, and though unwilling, she knew the choice wasn't hers to make; had never been hers to make. Her father with no face and every face nodded, and she stepped forward.

She woke lying face down in the book. One of the crushed pages had left a mark across her cheek. She still had half her list to complete. This time, as she hurried to complete her list, he didn't startle her. He sat at the center of the Archaeology section like before. But now he stood out, a greek among dinosaurs; his gold jersey emblazoned with crimson greek letters across every empty space. Stubble had replaced the sheen on his shaved head.

"I almost didn't recognize you without the black."

He looked both at her and through her. He stood as he had before and gathered his things.

She didn't know why she needed to keep him there, but the thought of watching those Greek letters receding moved something at her center.

"Don't leave."

He placed a yellow legal pad into a backpack.

"Guess it all worked out for you."

He zipped the backpack closed.

"The party. The chain."

He placed the straps across his shoulders.

"I hope I didn't make it harder for you. I was trying to help you carry it. The chain."

He stopped. "That was you?"

Vi nodded and sat down at the table.

He looked toward the exit sign, removed his backpack from his shoulder, and sat back down. He pulled the legal pad back out and began to write again as if she'd disappeared with his identification of her.

She watched him write without lifting his pen or looking up. "Are you writing a paper?"

He stopped writing as if he just realized she was sitting across from him. "No."

"A book."

"No." He looked up from the notebook. "A letter."

"To who?"

"To whom. My father."

"Does your father like words?"

"No." He placed his #2 pencil into the crease of his legal pad. "Actually he likes to brag that he's a man of very few words."

"Then why are you giving him so many?"

He looked at her as if sharing an inside joke to an insider. "Because I like words.

"You could have fooled me."

He laughed then. Not a full laugh. He laughed like someone not used to laughing. It reminded Vi of her attempts to express hopefulness when she first reached campus. The sides of his mouth softened. "You like words?"

She nodded, suddenly unable to claim any words for herself.

"Your favorites?"

"Diasporic condition. Imagined community. Familial legacy."

He laughed again. "What does any of that mean?"

"Nothing and everything."

He nodded as if he understood, and something inside of Vi lifted. "Are you hungry?"

"Yes."

"Can I feed you?"

The thought of the baby and her unrelenting hunger flashed into Vi's mind, but she still responded with only a moment's hesitation. "I have to take the cart back first. Will you wait?"

He nodded.

Vi grabbed Locke's book and the entangled cart, but left Brenda E. Moon's Myceneans behind. When she emerged from the Attic, the boy was waiting for her. She almost thought she'd dreamed it, but she hadn't. They walked to Skinner's Chicken Stand at the bottom of the hill. Ironically, their mutual love for words became swallowed in silence the moment they sat down across from each other. He ordered a chicken dinner for two, and once they'd rendered the remains to bones, she spoke again. "Why did you pledge?"

"For my father."

"You must love your father very much."

He shrugged. "Can you love something you don't know?"

She laughed. "Of course."

"Of course? Of course. Would you like to hear my letter?"

She nodded.

He read:

> Father,
>
> I hope you are well. I have done what you wanted. I have crossed the burning sands. I am branded G-Nu. I have fulfilled your legacy. I hate it here. I miss my room, my home, and mother. I don't like it here. I don't know the people. They don't know me. I don't like it here. I have done what you wanted so please send me back to where I was before I was here. Send me back. I want to do what I was doing before what I am doing now. It is hot here. Very hot and I don't like hot places. Send me back to where I was before I was here. How is mother? Is she still away? I would like to be away with her. Send me back to where I was before I was here. I do not belong here. I do not

belong here. These people are foreign to me. I am foreign to these people. They smell different. They talk different. They eat different food. They read different books. Send me back to where I was before I was here. I REMEMBER. No matter how long I am here I will never forget. My memory is long. Longer than any amount of time you can keep me away. I remember mother's face. I remember my room. I remember my home. I remember. Please send me back to where I was before I was here.

With the love of a son to his father,
Perrion Alabaster Cannon VII

Vi didn't know what to say. She understood wanting to go back. But Before was already gone. There could be no return, but she didn't want to be the one to tell him that. She didn't want to see his face go back.

"Perrion the Seventh. You're one of seven." She breathed sound into what she had known in soundlessness.

"Call me Perry."

"My name is Viola Ikewke Moon. One of one. Call me Vi." She sucked on a chicken bone. "So your father asked you to pledge?"

"No. He didn't have to ask. I just knew he wanted me to." He lit a match and touched it tenderly to the edge of his letter. "Our family history is well-documented." He said it with another man's voice and face. "We have been a part of north Georgia for centuries. In Albany for the last hundred." They both watched as the page turned blue and then red and then black, crumbling onto the table.

"That must be wonderful. To be born into so many."

His first face and voice returned. "To know my great grandchild's name before I know my child's mother." He took a bite of Vi's chicken. "It doesn't feel wonderful. It feels like a cage."

"If it's a cage, why do you want to go back?"

He shrugged. "It's where I'm from."

"Where you are from." She understood.

They walked back to his room in Lincoln's Hall and without asking she went in with him. She reached for his arms to place them around her, and he cringed. Before she could steady herself to back away, he grabbed her arm. He pulled the jersey over his head with one hand, exposing a block of white gauze across his heart that was seeping pink. She dug at the edges of the tape, and by instinct, he moved away and then back toward her. She didn't want to remove anymore of what the Gamma Nus had already taken, but she had to see what lay across his heart. It was pink and wet. The greek symbols that were emblazoned across his jersey had burned through to his chest. Vi kissed it. He shrunk back.

"It won't heal covered up." She knew scars. She took off her shirt and placed his hand on the question mark circling her breast. "Nothing between us. "

"Nothing between he us," he repeated, pulling her toward him.

After, she slept. No baby. No drowning. No tears. Just sleep.

She waited outside of Dr. Dotherightthing's office. He wanted to see her. She revised the Moon paper and resubmitted it, or more accurately, Ronnie revised the paper, but wasn't that the same? Weren't they the same? Vi felt good. The drowning baby had not visited for two nights, but Perry had. Maybe it had all been a very very bad dream and not the something more she initially imagined. Like last summer, hadn't all the doctors been right? She'd been so sure the cure was to remove them. So sure, she'd been willing to bet her life on it. Maybe she was wrong about the baby too. Maybe the child was as imagined as her cancer had been. She hadn't seen the baby again, so maybe it was all moot. Moot. One of Perry's favorite words. She smiled at the memory of him. The door to Dr. Dotherighthing's office finally opened.

"Hi Professor."

"Just call me Dr. Dotherightthing.

She laughed before she could stop herself. So he wasn't as self-involved as Vi assumed. She followed him inside the small office, surprised at the disorganized mess piled atop the desk. He seemed to be the kind of man to keep track of both the frequency and consistency of his bowel movements. When he waved her over to a spotless desk crammed into a corner, she realized she hadn't been completely wrong. He was both.

He followed her eyes to the messy desk. "I apologize. I'm a bit of a hoarder."

It must've been the other face's disorganized mess. The one who appeared for a moment the other day in class. The one he tried to keep hidden, like an evil twin. The invisible other's desk sat stacked with the likes of *Mama Day* and *100 Years of Solitude*. Emptiness took the place of things on the desk Dr. Dotherightthing chose to sit behind. It reminded her of her own once shared space; Danielle's excess and her emptiness.

"Viola, do you have your first draft?"

"Vi. And yes I do." She handed him the single-spaced diatribe, now more red than black and white. The F seemed even larger and redder as he flipped through the pages.

"Honestly." He sat back in his chair. "I thought your first draft much more interesting."

"Is that what the F meant?"

His lips bent at the corners, but no teeth. "The F was a reflection of the structure, not the content. Your ideas, when I could grasp them, were compelling." He pulled out her and Ronnie's paper. "This is almost the opposite. Structure with little to no compelling content."

"You're greedy." The veil rose, displaying her disdain.

"Pardon me." He blinked either toward clarity or as a warning.

In the little crammed corner space, sitting across from a controlled twin of himself, Vi didn't feel the need to run from her true thoughts. "No one can have everything."

"I'm not sure what you mean Ms. Moon. I don't want…"

"Everything. You want brilliance, but you want it dumbed-down. Brilliance doesn't adhere to structure. Some things simply can't coexist."

The corners of his mouth began to move again. Was he baring his teeth at her? "That's the voice that's missing from your second draft."

"I changed it because that voice got an F."

His mouth flew open then. Laughter, big, booming, and out of control. Never would she have imagined it coming from this controlled man. Maybe from the face that had appeared for a moment as he looked past her in class, but not this face sitting across from her. "You have an excellent point. If you would've submitted your second draft first, you probably would've gotten an A out of the box. But your first paper intrigued me, and this simply doesn't. Where is the inherent lie of written histories? The impossibility of a concrete truth? You couldn't move past them in your first draft."

"Does any of it matter? How do you really write about any of it? History is not a thing. It's a specific place at a specific moment in time. It's gone. You can't raise the dead. The past is completely and utterly unrecoverable."

"But does that mean we abandon its analysis?"

"I don't know, but I do know that an analysis doesn't stop—repetition, so what's the point. We only have now.

This closed man's face flew wide open, reaching for understanding that Vi did not feel able or qualified to give him. Why didn't she take one of Ronnie's pills before this meeting?

"That's where you lose me. Your argument becomes circular. It keeps returning to an indistinct beginning."

"Isn't that what everything does? Don't we all end where we started? And if we do, what's the point of looking back. We will all end there eventually. That's why you teach what you teach? The histories of our people? The patterns? You're really teaching us about ourselves, about this moment, right?"

He laughed that uncontrolled laugh again and nodded his head up and down. He wrote something across the top of the paper.

She looked down at the A in red. He understood? "Does this A stand for Acquiescence?"

His full-faced laughter followed her out of his office.

She didn't want to want it, but the A felt good in her hand. She had gotten it without hiding her true self. She needed to find Ronnie. His terrible paper had been key in Dr. Dotherightthing's recognition of her first paper. Ronnie liked to sit at the center of Booker T.'s Four Fountains and pretend he was the fifth, spewing revolution instead of stale water, so she headed toward Booker T. As she crossed at the Center, she saw him/them. Perry and his frat brothers moving as if one six-headed, red and gold snake with arms and legs. Perry stood as the head. Booker T.'s majestic projections leaped over their heads. The same compulsion she'd felt the day she'd almost broken the chain bubbled up inside of her. The red and gold snake pushed others out of its path, but she stood ready to assert her newly-discovered strength. Was that a Super A she'd just received on her paper? Did it make her impenetrable to testosterone-fueled snakes? Perry stopped a foot from her. He looked up into her smiling face before dropping his eyes and slithering straight toward her rooted feet.

Was she invisible to him? Had she imagined him? Them? Had he ever really fed her?

"Are you blind? Move!"

"Ju stop."

That voice broke the legacy's spell on Vi. As she turned, inadvertently stepping out of the path of the Gamma Nu snake, Danielle and Juju appeared. He stood inches away from Vi as Danielle's small hand clutched at his arm. Before she could form a response to a question she wasn't sure she'd been asked, Perry's voice rang out over all of them.

"Tittie in my mouth and ass in my hand, nobody fucks like a Gamma Nu man. But if I die before I come, leave your legs spread open so my frat can get some."

The remainder of the snake repeated the cadence.

"Danielle you need to tell your girl that when she sees the G-Nus coming through, she better make room."

Vi didn't see the look of apology in Danielle's eyes as she passed, still clinging to the arm of the bald black greek man because her eyes remained glued to the back of Perrion Alabaster Cannon VII's head. Did his father share that wrinkle above the nape of his neck?

Long fingers suddenly blocked her view from behind. With one sense blocked, the legacy's words moved toward her center. His disavowal rang in her ears as she imagined him being swallowed whole by the collective of the red and gold. She turned to Ronnie's face.

His eyebrows moved together. "Are you okay? Did those chocolate Neanderthals do anything to you?"

Vi pulled Ronnie in the opposite direction of the angry-faced man, her Danielle, the legacy and sat him at the center of the fountain. "We got an A." She handed him the crumpled damp sheets that just moments before had been proof of her power.

"Dr. Dotherightthing did the right thing." A strange expression played at the corners of his lips. "Damn. We must celebrate."

Celebrate. "Celebrate?" Vi tried to push the snake out of her mind's eye and recapture the feeling of before; Dr. Bennett's acquiescence. "I don't feel like..."

"Trust me Poorchild."

Trust? She couldn't even trust her own eyes and ears. How could she trust Ronnie? But she pretended to and followed him to the parking lot. She kept pretending as he unlocked the door of a sky-blue Pontiac Pinto that had seen much better days. She stopped pretending when the car refused to start after two tries.

Ronnie laughed in response to her obvious distrust. It reminded her of Dr. Dotherightthing's laugh. Not because it was the same, but the way they both echoed a contradiction. Though small and controlled, Ronnie's laugh filled up the rusted sky on wheels. "I know she's a piece of shit, but she's mine. Blue Thunder." The car violently coughed and roared into drive, reiterating Ronnie's christening.

Vi thought the name too much for the car to live up to. "Please tell me where we going?"

He parted his lips in a whisper. "Quincy."

She didn't recognize this tight-lipped version of Ronnie. "What is Quincy?"

"My hometown. I never told you I was from Quincy? Now sit back and enjoy the view."

Tallahassee was no Chicago, but compared to Quincy it might as well have been a bustling metropolis. Preplanned housing developments and strip malls quickly dissipated into mobile homes and emaciated horses as they entered the unincorporated township. It wasn't long before they were alone on the narrow two-lane highway. Evergreens canopied both sides of the winding road, and at times Vi doubted Blue Thunder could fulfill the task Ronnie had set before her. Before Vi had solidified her argument for returning to campus, they turned onto a gravel road.

Ronnie lowered the volume on the radio that had been blasting mostly static for the last two miles. He nodded toward a small neat clapboard home about half a mile off the gravel road. "Don't want to disturb Crazy

Mary."

"What?" Vi inspected the house for anything that would suggest a crazy woman abided within it, but she saw no signs.

"Nothing." He shook his head and turned off the gravel road onto a red dirt road. "Here we go. Home sweet home."

For whatever reason she'd pictured Ronnie coming from something more average, a well-cared for split-level in the midst of a planned community. Instead they parked in front of a sprawling Victorian, sitting in the midst of fields of lush acreage. It was Southfork instead of the Roots revision she'd imagined. Nothing about Ronnie gave off the farm-raised country boy vibe.

An older man watched their approach from the sprawling wraparound porch. He stood once the cloud of Blue Thunder had settled, hugging Ronnie the way men hold on to those they cherish. "RJ? Mom didn't say nothing about you coming home today."

"It was a last minute thing Daddy. Momma in the house?"

"Where else she gone be?"

"This is my girl, Poor   Vi. Vi this is my Dad."

Vi looked at Ronnie. He shrugged. The man who bore no mark of relation to Ronnie, stepped forward and extended his hand, giving Ronnie a high five behind her back. Ronnie moved differently here; his voice deeper; his manner stiffer. Was this his genuine self, or was the one she'd loved first real? The smell of simmering pinto beans greeted them as they entered the house. Cecilia Before loved pinto beans served with chunks of sweet onion and thick slices of heirloom tomatoes. Walking into the memory made Vi's mouth water and the question mark throb.

Ronnie entered the house with casual familiarity. "Momma! Where you run off to?"

"Is that my baby Ronnie, screaming through my house like I never taught him better?" She came in as a bustle of warmth with her round face shining from heat and excitement. She grabbed Ronnie's face with both hands and kissed him on his forehead.

Ronnie blushed, avoiding Vi's amused eyes. "Sorry Momma. I just wanted you to meet my friend. Vi. This is my Momma, Ms. Esther."

"Vi?" She approached Vi with the same loving touch that she'd

SUMMER OF THE CICADAS

extended to Ronnie.

"Short for Viola ma'am." Vi didn't want Ms. Esther to release her from her warm soft arms.

But she did, and held Vi at arms length, inspecting her. "Viola. Now that's a strong name. Who carried it before you?"

"Ma'am?" Vi was unsure of how to answer.

"That there is a name been passed down. Who you named for?"

"My father's mother." That she was sure of.

She nodded her head in the way older woman do when acknowledging their obvious rightness. Ms. Esther walked into the kitchen, and they followed. She took an iron skillet out of the stove and placed it on a trivet shaped like a rooster. "You all just in time for supper. This cornbread hot out the oven."

Vi's stomach began to do flips. She hadn't anticipated the hunger awakened by this kitchen's familiarity.

"Not right now Momma. We about to go down to the Red Oak for a bit." Ronnie grabbed Vi's hand.

Vi wanted to snatch her hand out of his. She didn't want to go visit any oak tree. She wanted to sit down at this table in this warm kitchen and have supper with Mr. Ron and Ms. Esther.

"Okay baby. Take something cold with you. It's sure a hot one today."

"Yes ma'am."

Vi let Ronnie guide her out of the house. Blue Thunder didn't have AC and neither did Ronnie's parents' house, so she'd been out in the uncompromising Florida sun for longer than she'd ever been, and Ronnie led her past at least ten perfectly formed red oak trees before he opened an old gate and gestured for her to follow him. "Come on."

Vi pointed at the only thing that seemed to be from this century in the vicinity. "But the sign says no trespassing."

"Who you think put that no trespassing there? Come on Poorchild." Ronnie walked her through the cemetery, explaining the relation, temperament and circumstance of each inhabitant. He stopped suddenly in front of a relatively new headstone. "This is my grandmother Sue. Oooh she loved her some baby Ronnie, and I loved me some her." He got on his knees in front of her headstone, and looked up at Vi, waiting for her to follow suit.

Vi continued to stand. "I don't pray."

Ronnie didn't respond. He just pulled her down next to him. "Just ask Grandma Sue for what you want?"

"Ask who?"

"It doesn't really matter which one you talk to. Ask Grandma Sue, or Great Aunt Tara or Uncle Lucius."

"But they're all dead."

"I know, that's why you should ask them. What good are ancestors if you can't ask them for something?"

"But these are your ancestors not mine. I don't have   people."

"Just because your daddy's dead don't mean you don't have people. Ask your daddy?"

"I lied. I'm not sure if my father is dead."

"Dead or alive, he's still your people. I haven't talked to my mother in years, and that doesn't stop me from coming out here."

"What do you mean you haven't talked to your mother? Who was that sweet imposter I just met?"

"Momma Esther is my stepmother. She helped Daddy raise me after my mother left us." Ronnie closed his eyes and pressed his palms together. "See. Anybody can be your people. All you need is two willing souls. And Momma Esther and me were both willing."

"You're lucky, you know that."

"If I am, then you are. What's mine is yours Poorchild." He waved his hand over the cemetery stones.

"What an inheritance." Vi laughed, and Ronnie shoved her, so she had to readjust in the rocky grass. Her knees were beginning to hurt, and she figured it would be easier to pretend and be able to get up and out of this place and back to Ms. Esther's warm hands and hot-buttered cornbread.

Ronnie rolled his eyes up in his head. "Just ask them. What can it hurt?"

He might be right. What could it hurt? So she mimicked Ronnie, pressing her palms together. She spoke into them the way she used to when she was still too young to doubt if anyone was listening. She thought of asking for the return of Cecilia Before but stopped. That would be too much for any borrowed dead ancestors on the first go round. She decided to make it smaller. Perry at the head of the snake. Bring Perry back to me. Bring Perry back to me she repeated again without sound. She opened her eyes to see Ronnie watching her, smiling.

"Good Poorchild. You'll see. Grandma Sue and them does not play. You'll see."

By the time Ronnie dropped her back in front of Tubman's Tower, she had talked herself out of Ronnie's faith in the power of ancestors, and into her new belief in southern cooking and hospitality. Ms. Esther's cooking settled easily in her stomach, her disbelief in Ronnie's ancestors shifted to the edges of belief when she saw Perry standing at the foot of Tower D, but as usual her eyes couldn't be trusted. A cloud shifted and the shadow she imagined to be Perry dissipated. Climbing the stairs to the second floor full and tired, her disbelief remained steadfast at her back.

She awoke to screams. It took a moment to recognize them as her own. The child had come back. This time she saw her face clearly. A tiny version of Cecilia. Something hit the window as she wrapped her arms around herself to stop shaking. Something hit the window again. This time harder, more purposeful. She padded toward the noise, still trembling and hugging. She pushed the window open and leaned forward to see him, staring up at her waiting, just as she'd imagined he would be when she kneeled down in the cemetery and spoke into her hands.

"I've been out here for an hour." He had on one of those golf shirts that people never played golf in.

"Can you see me?"

He nodded.

"Are you sure you can see me?"

"Yes. I see you."

"Was I invisible by the fountains?"

"Can I talk?" He pulled his legal pad out of his book bag. "I have the words to explain right here. Please let me read it to you."

She wanted to say no, but she couldn't. It seemed the architects of the tower had factored in apologetic lovers because Perry climbed to the second floor breezeway easily. Vi sat on Danielle's old side of the room, while he sat on her bed and began to read:

I am not what I pretend to be, so that means I can never stop pretending. I am not what I pretend to be, so if I stop pretending they will know and I will be stuck in between here and there. I cannot return to there so I am stuck here and if I am stuck here I must pretend. I was only pretending earlier. I could never not see you. I could never not see you. Please understand to be here I must pretend. I have no choice. We have no choice. We can both pretend. We can both pretend. With my sincerest regards. Your friend Perry.

By the time he reached sincerest regards Vi had already pushed his words from earlier to before. She extended her hand and he took it. They laid down together on the abandoned side of 203D. When he held her, the trembling stopped. Nothing stood between them and the small thin mattress. Vi felt the individual springs collapse against her backside as he pushed himself inside of her. He winced as his barely healed brand rubbed against her. She woke up from a dreamless sleep on Danielle's side of the room alone. Even though Perry had left her, she knew the parting had been painful because the bulk of the scab from his branding remained stuck to her chest.

CHAPTER SEVEN

They made the ride back in silence. Cecilia couldn't remember a time before a multitude of meanings tumbled between mother and daughter. It seemed they cut off her ability to understand her child alongside her breasts.

"How do you feel?"

Cecilia understood the words, but couldn't reach under them to get to the center like Before. Without knowing Vi's true meaning, how could she respond? "Fine."

"Fine? Good."

Only words to Vi, true understanding lost. Cecilia wanted to tell Vi to turn around and take her back to the hospital. She didn't give them permission to take this. She didn't authorize the erasure of what had flowed between her and her child.

"You'll let me know if you need anything, won't you?" Vi spoke as if talking to a distant acquaintance.

"Of course I will. Don't worry. I'll be fine." Cecilia watched Vi's profile for any sign of understanding. The heart that once pumped life for both of them still existed, beating underneath the bandages, stitches and scars. Cecilia needed Vi to hear all of it, but Vi kept her eyes on the road and hands on the wheel at ten and two. Maybe this was better. If Vi understood her, what would she do with that understanding? Would she still leave in less than a year? Probably not. It would be easier for Vi if Cecilia kept her meaning to herself. She got accepted into her top choice; A&M University. She would be so far from home, but the distance might be good for both of them. There was no longer any way for Vi to drown in her mother's milk. Her breasts had been removed with the cancer, so the dream was moot. Vi would have to be her own woman. She was now officially and irretrievably a bottle baby. Cecilia laughed like Before. Vi stopped the car. Did she understand? Did she hear it all in the laugh? Vi pulled the car into the garage. They were home. The laugh didn't mean anything to her second chance child. She didn't hear anything but an escape of air. The doctors cut it all away.

"Are you hungry?"

"No. I can't keep anything down. I think I just want to sleep for a few days."

The child looked concerned.

"The homecare nurse will be here soon." Cecilia smiled uneasily in an effort to erase the concern, but the look remained.

Vi helped her climb into bed before moving hesitantly toward the bedroom door.

"You can stay. Like Before."

"I don't want to." Vi's eyes moved toward the bandages hidden from view by Cecilia's nightgown. "Hurt you."

"Just sleep at my back."

The child hesitated again, so Cecilia held out her hand, and she took it. "We'll be fine."

Stillness hanging over the crib alarmed her. Cecilia held the baby in her arms like before. The child's head moved to the right, rooting before finally latching on, but no milk flowed. She tried to unlatch the child, but couldn't. A scream blossomed in her gut, behind her navel. The echo of the child's dry suckling could be felt in every bone of Cecilia's body. The stuck scream traveled up into her throat with each painful tug at her flaccid breast, until the baby's screeching frustration and hunger burst through like an overtaxed levy. Cecilia woke with shooting pains in nipples that no longer existed. She bit her lip to keep from screaming the scream scratching at the base of her throat. Vi continued to sleep, but her irregular breathing signaled to Cecilia that she shouldn't be here. Cecilia remembered the man she loved in the day and cursed in the night. He left. Vi shouldn't be here. Cecilia shook her, and Vi woke too suddenly. Cecilia hadn't meant to alarm the child, but didn't know how not to.

"Go to your bed."

"What?" Vi sat up in the bed somewhere between sleep and wakefulness.

"Go to your bed. You're almost seventeen. Time you learned to sleep alone."

"But."

"But nothing. Viola Moon get out of my bed." Her second chance child left the room cloaked in sleep and confusion. Cecilia needed Vi to be in front of her, not behind her. The only thing behind her was pain, and the only person who ever tried to stand next to her, left, and never came back. She couldn't risk losing Vi forever. This was Ellington Moon's child, but she wouldn't let her follow the same path.

CHAPTER EIGHT

She walked into her sociology class, easily connecting the low rumbled sound to meaning. Ronnie sat in the midst of the rumbling signifiers, radiating light like the cartoon depictions of power lines. When Dr. Bennett entered the classroom, the wattage increased, forcing Vi to look away.

"Good Afternoon. Today we're going to discuss the Black man, specifically the African American man. DuBois spoke of a double consciousness. Can anyone explain what he meant by that?"

Ronnie's hand shot up with a fierceness he had heretofore saved for extracurricular revolutionary activities. "DuBois was referring to the way in which blacks viewed themselves. They had to pretend to be one thing in front of white folks, and they were something else to themselves. Two-faced."

"Right. DuBois suggested this two-facedness forced a burden on the African American male which didn't exist for the white male or even the African male. Can you imagine the consistent strain of having to double think every move, every word, every thought. The strain of leading a double life has to manifest, and these manifestations are most clearly identifiable when one compares the divergences between the African male and the African American male. Does anyone know what the most distinct divergence is?"

No one offered a response.

"Homosexuality."

Giggles erupted across the room.

"No class this is very serious. Homosexuality is one of the most catastrophic manifestations of racism for the black male."

Ronnie's light stuttered and buzzed like a fluorescent tube fighting to stay lit. She wanted Dr. Bennett to shut-up, so Ronnie's light would come back on, but he kept talking.

"Homosexuality is not an African phenomenon. It is a European construction that black men have been seduced by. Homosexuality can be directly attributed to racial psychosis. It's America's psychological warfare at its best."

Vi waited for Ronnie to launch into the diatribe he had been preparing his entire life to deliver, but instead he sat frozen, trapped in voicelessness.

"The gay Black male is an emasculated black male whom has internalized that emasculation. A man belongs at the head of his family."

Again she waited for Ronnie to say something, trying to recall the words he had verbalized over and over to her.

"The Africans didn't have a word in their language for homosexuality. It is an American construction. In short it's the American construction of the perfect nigger."

She opened her mouth to respond in his stead, but couldn't. Vi knew the professor was lying, but it wasn't the lie she'd been preparing to defend against her entire life. She had only her own words, and they weren't good enough.

Then Ronnie left. He placed his books and notebook in his backpack and walked out of the classroom. A collective white noise followed Ronnie's departure.

Vi remained in her seat. Revolution required solidarity, not solitude. But she could finally see the light at the end of the tunnel; finally, felt she had a handle on how to survive in this place. When class officially ended, she wandered into the quad, and meaning cut through sound.

"Crazy Bitch."

She still got it every now and then. Usually one of the G-Nus, like this time; another Man of the Red and Gold. Like elephants, they never forgot, and she wanted them to forget. She tried to cut them off from their rememory by breaking the chain. She attempted to sacrifice all for one. Two unthinkable and unforgettable acts. She'd messed with a part of them that existed outside of memory. She was beginning to understand what lay at A&M's foundation. It might as well have legs and arms and breath. But if she intended to survive here, she needed that rememory to at least fade, and walking out with her gay best friend would not facilitate that sort of forgetfulness. She tried to imagine where he would have run to because she'd never seen him run. She walked through his dorm's parking lot, spotting Ronnie alone in Blue Thunder's passenger seat. He seemed smaller. Vi climbed into the driver's seat.

She drummed her fingers against the worn steering wheel and adjusted the Christmas tree shaped air freshener on the rearview mirror. "Where'd you go?"

"Here."

"I mean before you left. Where'd you go when he said those things?"

Ronnie shrugged, but the weight making him look smaller didn't fall from his shoulders.

"I don't understand. It was like. You weren't yourself. You would never let anyone, not even Dr. Dothe..."

"Please stop."

She fiddled with the controls on the radio, unsure how to console the consoler. "Are you hungry?"

He rocked his head from side to side.

"My treat. Skinner's two piece."

"Not this time."

This stranger scared Vi. "Just tell me where. I'll take you wherever you want to go." Grasping the steering wheel, the cracked vinyl bit into the tender part of her palm. She hid her discomfort by plastering an equally terrifying grin across her own face.

Without even looking at her, Ronnie open his car door. "If only that were possible." The Christmas tree shaped air freshener swung wide when the door slammed, releasing dying wisps of canned vanilla.

She wandered back toward General Lee's Hall, searching for Perry. She knew his schedule better than her own. He appeared almost nightly outside of her window like a black moon. Sometimes all of him, and sometimes chewed away at the edges, but always when she needed him to pull her back from the abyss of her night terrors. General Lee's halls stood empty. Classes hadn't been dismissed yet, so she sat on the stairs and waited until throngs of bodies began to move from one class to the next.

"Can I feed you?"

Was it divine intervention? Her full lips spread wide across her face. "Of course."

The answer came before Vi opened her mouth and in another girl's voice, but by the time she willed herself to turn, she could only see their backs. Perry's hand rested easily on the small of the girl's back, guiding her out of the door. Was she imagining things? Was she both abandoned and reclaimed? Was it possible to be both? No. The voice didn't belong to Vi. The girl with Perry wasn't Vi. She ran to catch up with them. Perry and the girl walked together like two halves reunited. They stopped by Booker T.'s Four Fountains, strolled past DuBois' Lane, and rested on the steps of Truth's Hall. He pushed her hair from her eyes. They embraced in the way people in love embraced. Was he pretending? Vi couldn't see his eyes. Or was he pretending, when he would crawl through her dorm window at night? She moved closer in an attempt to see his eyes and to be more sure about this man that was her future. Perry and the girl that was not Vi descended the steps of Truth's Hall and headed down the hill to the place where he fed Vi first. They walked past the evergreen shrubs that had been cut and sliced and trimmed out of their natural form into an A and a M and a U. When she attempted to follow, sound stopped her. The shrubs began to cry. She opened her mouth to call out to Perry, but couldn't place the appropriate words next to each other in a way that would convey what she needed from him; the crying shrubs hid a secret, her family secret, and only through his body, his name, his legacy, was the child fed. Even if she could find the words, he wouldn't understand. He would think she was crazy like everyone else. He was too busy building his own imaginary self. That girl, like the red and gold he wore across his back and burned into his chest, could only be a prop; an imagined construction. Vi knew that, but it didn't erase the fact she could hear the baby from behind those sheared evergreens in the middle of the day. Once a nightmare. Now a ghost. Vi thought Perry had made the child's hunger moot; chased her back into the nether regions of a long forgotten history. But the baby's reached was growing instead of waning, as Perry climbed down the hill with another girl. She needed to talk to Cecilia.

— Cecilia?

— How have you been?

— Well. You?

— Fine.

—

— Are you still there? What's wrong?

—

— Vi?

— I'm still here.

— Are you okay? What's wrong?

— I heard her today.

— Who?

— Your baby.

— Vi stop it. You are my baby.

— I mean the one you had before me.

— What? Baby, what are you talking about?

— The baby. She's back and I don't think she's going away this time.

— Vi. Please stop.You're scaring me.

—

— Vi?

— Yes Cecilia.

— I'm going to call Dr. Gabrielle, and call you right back. Stay by the phone.

—

— Vi? Will you wait there for me?

— For you. I'm going to hang up now, but I'll be here when you call back.

Vi put the phone back in its place, with no intention of waiting. Dr. Gabrielle belonged to her broken fragmented past; her Before. Vi belonged here in this place now, in this place steeped in history and tradition, a place she had not known belonged to her. Cecilia hadn't figured it out. Wouldn't admit her mistake; her failure. Cecilia chose the wrong man, a man with no name, no fathers. Why should she wait for Dr. Gabrielle? What did she know anyway?

— *Tell me about your father.*

—

— What happened to him?

— Nothing happened.

—

— He just left.

— Do you ever discuss it with you mother?

— Why? Gone is gone.

— You don't think it matters if he left because of circumstances out of his control.

—

— Vi?

— Circumstances are always beyond control.

—

— He couldn't have saved us anyway.

— Saved you from what?

—

— Vi? Save you from what?

— What does this have to do with my cancer?

— What cancer?

— My breast cancer. The reason I'm in this hospital.

— Vi you don't have breast cancer.

— How do you know? You haven't even examined me.

— No. I'm not that kind of doctor. But I talked to your other doctors, and they assured me you don't have cancer.

—

— Why are you so sure you do?

— Because Cecilia does.

— What do you mean?

— I mean she has it, so I must.

—

—

— Viola you do know that you and your mother are two separate individuals.

—

— Vi?

— Of course. Dr. Gabrielle. I'm not a moron. Of course I know that.

Vi would not repeat Cecilia's mistake, but she shouldn't have called Cecilia. She redialed the numbers.

— Cecilia?

— Vi?

— I'm sorry. I shouldn't have called you the first time. I just had a bad dream and woke up confused.

— I understand.

— I'm still getting used to sleeping alone.

— Alone? What about your roommate?

— It's not the same.   Are you okay?

— Me? Of course.

— I just don't want you to worry. I'm fine. Just a little tired.

— I wasn't able to get in touch with Dr. Gabrielle, but I left her a message. She'll be expecting a call from you.

—

— Vi?

— Yes.

— Get some rest.

— I will.

— I love you Vi.

— Me too.

A chill hovered inside of 203D. That girl Perry waltzed across campus was only a prop, so Vi wouldn't turn back, but she had to quiet the child somehow, at least for now. The two little blue pills stared at her from her desk drawer. They stuttered down her throat without water. Five minutes passed before for the child's cries dissipated, and Vi relaxed into the lonely bunk and closed her eyes. She had to be at the Attic soon, and she promised Cecilia she would rest.

When she entered the Attic everything either appeared out of focus or on zoom. Ronnie's pills altered her worldview in a way she didn't want to become accustomed to. The pills represented a temporary fix until she could reach Perry. The chill in 203D had followed her into the Attic. She grabbed her shoulders, rubbing them for warmth. Fluorescent lights buzzed a soft accompaniment to the inaction of the Attic. Dead and dying bugs sizzled between the cylindrical tubes. Had Dr. Locke always worn that threadbare corduroy blazer with the frayed sleeves? Was the lint peppering his black puffy hair a sign of his current deterioration or had it always been there? The clarity of her vision disturbed Vi; pushed her off balance like she remembered being in Chicago, before the cicadas. If clarity came only with Ronnie's pills, did that make her true self crazy? Tunisia stood next to the elevator, waiting for Vi to grab her cart and join her.

Dr. Locke raised his eyes in her direction. "New protocol Ms. Moon. You will be getting your control sheet directly from me." He held out the control sheet, but when she reached for it, he held onto it for a second longer than he needed to. "The pulls in the right left corner are to come directly to me. Do you understand Ms. Moon?"

She returned his conspiratorial tone with a nod. "Of course Dr. Locke. Just like last time."

His eyes moved in the direction of Tunisia, and he lowered his voice so it would not bounce off the hard walls. "Exactly. Just like before."

Vi moved into the elevator with Tunisia and waited for the elevator doors to close before interrogating Tunisia. She could not trust her perception of Dr. Locke's departure from his usual strange behavior due to her own altered state. "Is he okay?"

Tunisia pressed her lips together in a false pout. "He's upset over a missing Control Sheet. He says he gave it to me, but I know he didn't. I don't know why he's tripping. What I want to steal a control sheet for? I got Control Sheets coming out of my ass." She pointed toward the opening elevator doors. "Ain't this you?"

Vi pushed the cart off the freight elevator. This also seemed new, like she had never been in this section of the library. She looked at her list. *The Mediterranean.* She should probably pull Dr. Locke's books first, but Locke's need was momentarily eclipsed by her sudden need to search for a Moon. This filtered clarity confused her. She needed to find solid ground to stand on. She needed to hold a Moon. Once she found one, she would be able to continue with her assigned task. So engrossed in the search, she almost didn't hear him come up behind her. As quietly as he approached, she could feel the strength of his bloodlines.

He stood behind her and pressed his erect penis against her backside, but she pushed back against him, pushing him away. He returned this time wrapping his arms around her waist, forcing his hot breath into her ear. "Nothing between us." She wanted to say no and yes at the same time. She wanted him inside of her to fill the place her ghost left, but not like this. But to deny him meant to deny her permanent solution. The drugs were only temporary, so she nodded and leaned over the empty cart. That girl he walked across campus meant nothing. He belonged to her as deeply as he thrust inside of her. The grunts emanating from somewhere deep inside of him sounded foreign. He sounded like one of those hungry shadow people Tunisia displayed the first day? Something separated from the shelf in front of her, but the shadow disappeared as quickly as it split. She pushed Perry away from her and pulled up her pants. She shook her head. "This isn't how it's supposed to be."

He pulled his pants up. "I won't pretend with you." He picked up his book bag and walked away.

Perry was gone, but she could still feel him behind her, pushing against her, needing her to feed him as much as she needed him. When she finished her pulls and headed back down to the Attic, Tunisia was already there, waiting. She showed Vi her teeth as she rolled her cart past her. "Nasty girl."

Vi stopped pushing.

The sick laughter from that first day echoed off the tall walls. "Who that singing that nasty song? Who that doing that nasty dance?"

The as yet silent Dr. Locke spoke. "Ms. Johnson, please refrain from making that horrible noise in my presence. I am trying to work."

"Sorry Dr. Locke. I just can't get that song out of my head. Vi what about you? Don't you just love that song?"

It was the type of question that didn't wait for an answer. Vi looked toward Dr. Locke for help, but he, of course, was marking a report.

"You've heard it. It's an oldie but goody. Janet Jackson. You know you've heard it."

"I'm not that much of a pop music person."

"I'll put it on my ipod tonight and let you listen to it tomorrow."

Vi looked back at Dr. Locke. He was still not watching her.

Tunisia left humming the song, and Dr. Locke put down his permanent magic marker.

Vi could smell Perry wafting from in between her thighs. Could Dr. Locke smell him too?

"Ms. Moon, my pulls?"

Vi stacked the books on the edge of the desk.

Dr. Locke slid them onto another cart behind his desk. "I hope you realize the isolation in this place is only imagined. There are eyes and ears all over the library, so be on guard."

"Yes sir." Had it been him splitting the dark in two in the middle of the Mediterranean?

"Overall you are doing a fine job, and with much less chatter than Ms. Johnson. But alas, I am unable to choose my staff. I must accept whomever ACPAC and Dr. Cristabel send me. But I digress. I would not want to lose you over a mistaken impression. You must mind your guard. There are greater forces at work in this place."

"I'll do my best. " She couldn't catch her breath in the stairway. Perry's smell engulfed her, like she'd been marked like a dog marks a tree. But it wasn't like that. Perry was not a dog. He was different, and he needed her as much as she needed him.

Nat Turner stood at the center of Lincoln's cold courtyard. White tulips bloomed at his bared bronze feet. She imagined Perry's face in place of Nat's. His people knew all of their own faces. They could recognize themselves in a crowd. They didn't have to check mirrors for reference. Perry knew his place without doubt. He was the seventh son. She waited for what seemed like hours, but it could have been minutes.

When he walked into the courtyard, he spoke as if he expected to see her waiting there. "Are you upset?"

She shook her head from side to side.

He walked past her to the dorm's side door and held it open. She climbed the steps behind him. "Vanessa is   . I don't want there to be anything between us."

Vanessa. The girl, whom he fed in her stead, was named Vanessa. "I know what she is."

"Nothing."

"Nothing."

He picked jeans and socks and t-shirts from the floor and pushed them into an already overstuffed duffle bag.

"Are you leaving?"

"Going."

"Going where?

"Home."

"Home?" Should she tell him now there was no return; that going back was an impossibility.

"I want you to come with me."

The impossibility of return gave way to his ancestral legacy. He was one of many, and he wanted to take her home. The aching that sat at her center since she first saw him, the imagined Vanessa, and the real ghost began to throb. He wanted to take her home.

CHAPTER NINE

The first time Cecilia saw her like that, she didn't know what to think. She witnessed what seemed a preoccupation, a stage Vi was going through. Cecilia thought it a developmental reenactment, probably performed by most every teenage girl. She would catch Vi standing in front of the mirror staring at her bare breasts, not as if fascinated by the size and shape of them, but more of a clinical examination. Sometimes she would snatch glimpses of Vi with a ruler or measuring tape; sometimes Cecilia would see her scribbling down notes. It didn't seem to matter to Vi if the bedroom door stood wide open or not, often oblivious to anything other than the mounds on her chest. Cecilia couldn't remember any such fascination before her surgery, but maybe because so much silence didn't exist before and without the clutter of words and meaning, Cecilia simply became more watchful. Learning to trust the ocular proved to be a process. She'd always believed the visual more susceptible to misinterpretation than sound, but the surgery changed that belief. But this time, the vision of her second chance child erasing her breasts in front of the bathroom mirror gave pause. This time Vi wrapped her chest so tightly with not-her-flesh colored bandages that the child struggled to exhale, and still she didn't seem to notice Cecilia standing behind her. The mirror reflected back a two-headed woman with four arms and no breasts. As Cecilia unwrapped the binding, a map of small welts rose across Vi's breasts, recording the temporary erasure. The reflection of Vi's eyes followed the bandages as they tumbled onto the tile floor.

"You are beautiful. Why are you hiding?"

Vi pushed up her shoulders and covered her now bare breasts with her forearms. "I don't know."

"Vi. Please. Talk to me."

The reflection of her daughter pulled away from her, and they became two separate women again. "They will kill me, just like they killed…"

"Me?" She grabbed Vi's hunched shoulders and turn to see her face to face. "But I'm right here Vi, and I'm fine."

"You're right." She bent down to pick up the puddle of bandages on the floor. "I don't know what came over me."

Cecilia watched Vi's bare back retreat down the hall and into her bedroom, closing the door quietly behind her.

CHAPTER TEN

Twisted black iron announced Albany's town limits. A warning more than a welcome. A city of ghosts. Just a mile outside of the city limits Vi spotted the child in the middle of Highway 319. She screamed. Perry slammed on the brakes, but there was no one there. A raccoon on its hind legs surprised into action by the approaching headlights. Not her ghost. She re-upped with Ronnie before the trip, determined to leave her ghost on A&M's campus until—Until a more permanent solution could be found. Though Vi's ghost stayed gone for the rest of the drive into Albany, her anxiety continued to grow as the arrival at Perry's birthplace became inevitable. Towns like Albany negotiated a feigning peace, behaving as if centuries of pain left nothing behind. How could a place where the sons and daughters of torturers and the tortured intermingle not have some sort of residue? The residue remained like sludge after dried-up floodwaters, sediment under manicured Kentucky bluegrass, sitting, waiting, seeping. Perry's face changed when they crossed Albany's town limits. The half-openness Vi had become accustomed to closed completely. As Perry pulled his car into the circular driveway, his closed face alarmed her. The feeling of the house unsettled her in a way she hadn't been since leaving Chicago.

"Wait here." He disappeared behind the double doors, leaving only a small opening. "Mother. Mother." Silence encircled Perry's cry as the echo bounced back through the gap between the doors.

Vi followed the veranda surrounding the house. In the distance a woman sat under a towering sycamore and a less-towering black and white striped hat. Just beyond the hat stood a perfectly groomed wall of English hedges. A gardener, the source of the perfection, actively trimmed the already perfect-to-the-eye bushes under the woman's devout scrutiny.

"No one is home. They must be at the Club." Perry called from the now closed doors.

Vi didn't offer up what she'd witnessed from the veranda to Perry, instead she returned to the car in silence, relieved that her Cannonization would be deferred a bit longer.

As they circled back away from the house, Perry's gaze rested on the woman under the black and white hat without Vi's help. But instead of returning, he refocused on the road in front of him. "Would you prefer the scenic route?"

"Show me everything. I want to see where you're from."

Perry limited everything to anything he could point to from the most direct route to the Club. They arrived too quickly. The only sign that marked the Club as the Club were the twisted iron gates, replicas of the gates they'd passed to enter Albany's town limits. The Club, encompassed in white classical hardness, put one in the mind of the Parthenon but much further south. Marble columns alongside marble representations of Greek gods greeted them as they entered the main building's rotunda. Vi almost expected to be hailed by toga-donned servants. Perry made an excuse about men only and locating his father that Vi was too preoccupied to hear clearly, before disappearing behind a set of large mahogany doors. So distracted by the Club's inhabitants she barely noticed his departure. White and black both served and were served here side by side. Is this what Booker T. envisioned? Was this his fist? Were these men and women, who looked as if they stepped off the pages of a Ralph Lauren catalog, the fingers? As she stood under a reproduction of Icarus and his final flight on the rotunda's ceiling, she was reminded of her difference by the way both the servers and the served ignored her. She seemed to be cloaked under a cape of invisibility despite her external representation baring no marked difference from their own? They themselves represented a rainbow of hues. Was her historical disconnection that obvious? Perry reappeared as suddenly as he'd disappeared.

"Father is finishing up on the course. And Mother is not here. I must have missed her at the house." Before Perry could usher her back through the Grand Hall, a collective of the served approached. As the array of pastel golf shirts and chinos drew nearer, Vi wished herself back into true invisibility. Yet and still, a chubby brown piece stepped out of the collective and enthusiastically engaged Perry.

"Cannon. What's up man? I thought you were down at A&M?" His wide mouth revealed a slight gap between his bottom teeth.

"I am. Just home for the weekend."

"Heard you went over. A G-Nu man now." His mouth widened, and Vi tried to focus on the gap, but Perry's transformation distracted her. She blinked and by the time she reopened her eyes Perry disappeared, and in his stead stood the Gamma Nu Man. Chubby and Gamma Nu Man moved together into a half hug, and locked the fingers of their right hand in a series of movements purposefully hidden from her view.

Vi didn't mean to, but she stepped back. The only sign Perry gave that he noticed her movement, a momentary hesitation releasing Chubby's hand.

"And who is this?" The gap disappeared.

"This is Viola."

The piece of the clump extended its soft and sweaty hand, and Vi took it. It was soft and damp.

"This is your first time to Albany?"

Vi saw the question mark, but heard a declarative sentence. "Yes." She wanted to rub the sweat from the palm of her hand down the front of his stupid shirt and stuff his gap-toothed declarative questions into the space between his teeth.

"I hope our fine city is making you feel at home." His stance communicated the opposite.

"Of course."

Gamma Nu Man spoke in Perry's voice. "Well I better get home. Mother will kill me if she knew I was gallivanting all over Albany before she's had the chance to lay eyes on me."

Neither one of them spoke until they were on the other side of THE CLUB's gates. "Did you see your father?"

G-Nu fell away as quickly as it had grown. "Yes."

The suddenness frightened Vi. How could anyone change so quickly and seamlessly; even Superman needed a phone booth. But she made a promise. If he couldn't show her all of his faces, what did they have? There could be nothing between them. "Did you tell him about me?" Had he told him she'd come for him? That she needed his people? She watched Perry's profile for a sign; something to clarify his practiced art of non-language.

"Yes."

"What did he say?"

"He said to tell mother he would be home late." His lips tightened.

She waited for more, but he offered nothing. "What about your sister?"

"Diana?"

"Was she at The Club?"

"Diana?" He snorted. "The Club is not a place she visits voluntarily." He turned toward Vi as if something had just occurred to him. "I need a drink. You want one?"

"Do you remember what happened the last time I had a drink?"

"Yes. You saved me.   I know a place. Don't worry. It's nothing like The Club. It's on the other side. The Brief Encounter. He seemed almost satisfied in that moment, and Vi wanted to delay the return to the Cannon house as long as she could. "To the Encounter."

He turned the car around and headed down a lonely two-lane highway. He turned without warning down a small dark dirt road. Vi hadn't seen any sign of a bar or restaurant. A small ramshackle structure appeared, awkwardly squatting in the center of a grove of overgrown sycamores. As he turned into the full lot, gravel crunched and popped under the tires. Soft lights twinkled on the building's sagging overhang. A clumsily painted sign arched across the black door announcing The Brief Encounter.

Perry stopped at the bar first. The bartender could've been forty or sixty. Missing teeth and smooth brown skin gave conflicting clues. "Hey Schoolboy, what can I get you?"

"Two rum and cokes."

"I ain't gone get in no trouble serving y'all?" The man's eyes focused on Vi's face.

"The only trouble you'll have is if you don't." Perry's voice held a welcome that didn't reach his eyes.

The crowd parted as Perry moved through them with the drinks.

Pats on the back and greetings from every side of the room suggested a camaraderie that didn't really exist on either side. The contact came begrudgingly and was accepted in the same vein. Perry sat her down at a table in the back, but even from the perimeter of the crowded dance floor, they remained at the center of the Encounter, interlopers slumming. Though they sat at a table for four, no one ventured to claim the only two empty seats in the packed club, or approach them. Their drinks seemed to refill themselves.

The music played too loudly for conversation, and Vi suspected that was at least one of the reasons Perry frequented this place. Closing his eyes, he leaned into the bass pumping through the worn speakers from across the scuffed floorboards.

Vi tried to relax with him but couldn't find a resting place in the disruptive bass. A cloyingly sweet scent interrupted her attempt. When Vi saw her, she suspected she'd located the other reason Perry haunted The Brief Encounter. The girl could've been plucked from prepubescent wet dreams. Everything about her suggested multiple ejaculations. When she moved, the Encounter moved. She leaned into the empty space next to Perry, completely ignoring Vi.

"Baby Boy. Dede didn't tell me you were home?"

Vi couldn't stop looking at the girl's breasts. The blouse she wore left more displayed than not. They looked like breasts built to feed a nation.

"Just got in." Perry's eyes followed Vi's. "You're looking good as usual."

"Thanks." She pulled out the seat in front of Perry and leaned even further into him, still not acknowledging Vi's presence, and exposing even more of her nation-building chest. "Buy me a drink?"

"Of course. Just tell A.D. you're on my tab. Like always." Perry leaned back in his chair and closed his eyes as the bass rose.

Without Perry's gaze, the girl shrank. Even her bosom seemed to shrivel. She adjusted the front of her blouse to account for the shrinkage and headed back in the direction she'd come from, disappearing into the pulsating crowd. The rum and cokes, the rising bass, mixed with the girl's sweet-smelling perfume made Vi's head spin.

She tapped Perry on his shoulder and mouthed the words more than she spoke them. "Where's the ladies room?"

Perry pointed to a dark corner, before closing his eyes and returning to the drums.

The restroom displayed no signage to indicate who could and could not enter, so Vi pushed through the door with the assuredness of one without choice. Plum peeling walls and cracked white and black tiles suggested The Brief Encounter's longevity. There were only two stalls. Her stomach churned. She swung the door of the first stall open, but stopped when she saw what the less than courteous previous visitor left floating in the tank. The sight and smell pushed the smells and sights of her previous interaction closer to the surface. The door in the second stall swung open easy until it hit the heel of a silver platform shoe. The shoe belonged to a foot attached to a leg supported by a knee pressed against the dirty black and white cracked tile. Vi covered her mouth.

"What the fuck." It came from the man leaned up against the stall wall, cradling the girl's head at the center of his thighs. His eyes bounced back and forth from Vi and the bobbing head girl, then rolled up into his eyelids. His body shook from the inside out, which must have eased his grip on the bobbing head, because it turned. Plum passion lipstick, smeared from the bottom of her nose to her top lip, mixed with the drying semen leaking from the corner of her mouth. Vi prepared herself to be cussed out, but instead the smeared, semen-encrusted lips spread, exposing two rows of perfect white teeth. "Learn anything?"

The rum and perfume bubbled up like a bottle of cheap champagne. Vi just made it into the unflushed stall. When she attempted to flush, she realized that the previous visitor had simply been abandoned by working plumbing. As the mixture of discarded wastes began to rise, Vi backed out of the stall. She managed to splash cold water on her face and exit just as what she left behind began to overflow and seep into the lovers' stall. She hoped the girl had made it off her knees.

Perry still sat alone when she leaned into his ear. "I'm ready to go."

He briefly pulled away from her before standing up. The stink of the restroom along side her contribution to that stink had obviously followed her. He moved quickly through the Encounter, as if he'd anticipated her need to flee.

They were headed back down the main road before Vi spoke. "Why did we go there?"

"It's where I go."

"Who was that girl?"

"Someone I used to see."

"She wasn't what I expected. For you."

"She's what they expect." His eyes referenced the landscape speeding past. "This is where I'm from."

"That's where you're from?" But you are one of seven.

He turned through another gate and parked the car without answering.

Footsteps echoed through the foyer. Vi looked over her shoulder more than once before finally realizing the footsteps were her own. She followed closely behind Perry as they passed portrait after portrait hanging from the wall.

Perry noticed her slowed steps. "My sister likes to call it Hangman Hall. Further proof of our backwardness. Once you die, you come here to hang."

"All of you."

He shook his head. "Only the carriers of the name."

"No mothers?"

He shook his head again.

She had no Hangman Hall; no record; no line of dead patriarchs to inherit. Only a forgotten baby. A sign of an unrecoverable past. What did she need it for anyway? Perry's past hung right here, prime for the picking. Surely he wouldn't mind sharing. Surely it's why he brought her here.

Perry placed his index fingers against his lips. "Mother is asleep by now. I'll take you to my room."

Vi followed. The emptiness of the house made it appear smaller than she imagined. For a moment Vi imagined how a real estate ad might mark the lack. "And this colonial is bathed in emptiness, plenty of room for the young family. Plenty of hidden corners and closet space for your own skeletons." She laughed and Perry turned momentarily before opening a door and signaling her to go through it. Vi entered a room of perfectly-staged artifacts. Each item appeared to have been chosen to reflect who Perry should've been. The crossed oars over the bed. The leather bound copy of *Tom Sawyer* on the desk. Even the marine blue walls felt like smoke and mirrors. "How did you breathe?"

"Like Moby." He pointed to a realistic rendering of Ahab and the Great White on the wall. "I held my breath."

Vi plopped onto the compass-covered comforter "Why do you want to come back to this?"

He shrugged. "Is school so different? At least this I know." He touched the whale on the wall. "Are you hungry?"

"No." Her stomach began to churn again.

He seemed to understand. "I'll get you some club soda. The bathroom is across the hall if you need it." He left her alone in his ancestral room.

Once she lay down, Perry's bed began to spin, so she placed one foot flat on the floor. Balance. The bed stopped spinning, and she closed her eyes.

Buzzing woke her. No. A whirring woke her. Behind her, close, but outside of her peripheral vision. She turned to visually define it and the sound turned with her. The room became a hallway. Closed doors lined both walls. The whirring propelled her forward. She turned the knobs of each door in the order of their appearance. The last one gave way into a room of mirrors, rendering multiple reflections of herself. The source of the whirring and catalyst for her movement—a pair of wings. Not the brilliantly feather testaments to God's strength, but small fat fluttering atrocities growing from the center of her shoulder blades. The mirrors only multiplied their freakishness. Perry, no, an image of Perry looked down from the mirror above her. Under her feet, the child. Behind her, in front of her, and at her sides, copies of copies of the fluttering at her back bounced back toward her. Suddenly, under the scrutiny of both Perry's and the child's reflections, one question climbed above all the others. Could she fly? A window appeared in the middle of one of the mirrored walls. She climbed up into the window well, and without looking up, down or back, she jumped.

"Are you okay?"

Vi opened her eyes. A face appeared above her, shaking her awake. Sunlight cascaded through the window onto Ahab's testimony on the wall. She reached over her shoulder. No wings. She was in Albany. In

Perry's room. In Perry's bed.

"I'm fine. A bad dream. Where's Perry?"

"Gone."

Panic flurried across Vi's face.

"Don't worry. He's coming back. He had a suspicion you might wake up with a headache, so he went to the drugstore. He'll be back shortly. Can I feed you?" The girl unleashed a dazzling smile. She had seen it before, but less open. It belonged to Perry.

"I'm Diana, the sister."

"I'm Vi." The what? Friend? Girlfriend? Lover? What was she in relation to Perry?

Diana pushed her lips together. "I'll let you get dressed. Come downstairs if you're feeling up to it, and we'll have brunch."

Vi didn't realize the depth of her hunger until she entered the kitchen. A short plump woman barely looked up from her perch at the kitchen island, acknowledging Vi's hello with a curt nod toward the patio doors. On the other side of the doors, Diana sat at a table covered with enough food to feed a family of ten, staring at the spot occupied by the woman with the black and white hat the evening before. Diana didn't notice Vi approaching.

"Diana."

She looked up and nodded toward the empty wicker chair across from her.

Vi sat down under Diana absentminded scrutiny. "So Vi, tell me about yourself. What does your father do?"

"My father's dead." Vi didn't know why she resurrected Danielle's lie, but saying it made it seem more real.

"I'm sorry to hear that. Your mother? What does she do?"

Vi shrugged. "She gets into her car, goes to a tall building, and comes back eight hours later."

"Sounds so normal." A mist traveled across the girl's face. "How does it feel to be normal?"

Vi wanted to laugh out loud, but instead she looked down at her empty plate. "You're definitely asking the wrong person."

Diana waved her hand over the feast. "Please help yourself. "

Vi filled a plate with sliced pineapples and honeydew melon.

Diana's eyes narrowed as she watched Vi bite into the pineapple. "Who are you?" The sweetness that had been covering her true nature, fell.

Vi dropped the pineapple, knowing only one way to answer. "I'm Viola Moon."

"Your people. Who are your people?"

"I have none. Just me and my mother." Vi could hear the fluttering of inadequate wings, but knew it was only an echo from her dream.

With lips covered in a glossy plum passion, Diana grimaced. "Finally the favored son rebels. It's easier than my method, but I'm sure infinitely less fun."

Since crossing Georgia state lines, she'd been terrified the signs would sever from the signifier and leave her trapped in a new place amongst strangers with no language, no comprehension, but just then, Vi wished for meaninglessness. Pushing the plate of acidic fruit back toward the center of the table, Vi stood. "I'm going to try to find something to settle my stomach."

Diana pulled her sweetness back up, stood up, and laced her arm through Vi's as she guided her back toward the kitchen. "Maybe we can get Li to whip up some of her special sweet tea. She makes the best tea in Albany?" Diana moved her hair from her face and leaned into Vi's ear. "I'm going to let you in on a little Cannon family secret. She makes it from the Lipton mix, but that's what we do here. Brag on our domestic's domestic ability. Be it real or imagined." She smelled like eucalyptus.

Vi prayed this girl would continue to play nice. She needed Diana to want her here, or at least do a much more consistent job of pretending. They stepped back into the kitchen with the woman who perched at the huge center island.

"She doesn't speak very good English. Mother prefers it. Says she doesn't have to worry about her gossiping to the neighbor's help. Isn't that right Li?"

In response to her name, Li looked up and nodded before returning to the latest issue of *Cosmopolitan* magazine.

Diana poured Vi a glass of Li and Lipton's sweet tea and motioned for her to sit in the chair across from her. Diana wasn't beautiful, at least not in the since of perfect symmetry, but she knew how the light hit her face. She understood the hairstyle that would most complement her facial structure. Her makeup was impeccably applied. Her sundress was cut to perfection to expose what worked and hide what didn't. Diana hid her non-beauty masterfully.

Footfalls in the foyer interrupted Vi's contemplation. She hoped they belonged to Perry. Her head still pounded, and she needed to be rescued from Diana's duplicity.

"Diana, Is that you? Can you bring your overheated father a tall glass of sweet tea?"

"Daddy come in here. There's someone I'd like you to meet."

Perry's father in the flesh stood right around the corner. The Sixth of Seven. Vi focused on connecting the voice with an actual physical body, but something in Diana's voice compelled Vi to turn back toward her. The feigned sweetness fell away, and Diana stood exposed with the need she'd hidden thus far on full display. The Sixth's voice and body fused under the kitchen's grand arch, and he finally stood in front of her, blood and bone. From Perry's words she'd constructed a giant, but this man disappointed, if only in his physicality. He stood at least a head shorter than Perry. He extended his hand toward her, and Vi hesitated, waiting for the ground to shake or lightning to strike. Something, anything to indicate the significance of the moment.

"Daddy this is Perry's girlfriend, Viola?" Diana turned toward Vi, waiting.

"Moon." If Vi hadn't been watching as intently as she always did, she would've never seen it. It was a hesitation, not more than a millisecond, and his left hand moved at the same moment in an attempt to distract. The Sixth was like any practiced magician who could keep any meaningful revelation masked by timely diversion, but what did it mean. Had he recognized her intention that quickly?

"Welcome Viola Moon. It is a pleasure to meet you. Where is Perry?"

"Viola wasn't feeling well, so he went to the drugstore for aspirin."

The Sixth turned toward Vi. "I hope you're feeling better.

Vi nodded, remembering his need for few words.

"Your mother?"

Diana nodded toward the stairs.

"Well no need to disturb her." He turned back toward Vi as she struggled to locate Perry in his face and mannerism, but his face revealed nothing. While Perry had learned to bluff on occasion, she could read him, but not the Sixth. "Apologies for our ragtag welcome, Viola, but I'm afraid Perry didn't inform us that you were accompanying him." He turned to go. "Diana, make sure Viola is made to feel at home."

"Of course Daddy." She beamed, but it had no affect on the Sixth. He'd already turned and headed up the stairs. With her need both unfulfilled and exposed, Diana refocused on Vi with renewed rancor. "So how did you meet my dear brother?"

Vi took a sip of tea. The lack of sugar and overuse of lemon juice stung the roof of her mouth. "At school."

"That's apparent, but how? You're obviously not a sorority girl, or a G-Nu Sweetheart. How exactly did you find yourself close enough to the inner circle to touch the hem of the chosen one's garment?"

Vi took another sip of the bitter tea. The second sip tasted less bitter than the first, or maybe she simply adjusted to the bitterness. "We met while he was on line."

Diana's perfectly shaped brow rose. "And the plot thickens. Do tell more."

Vi knew she shouldn't share the circumstances of her and Perry's meeting with this gorgeous/plain girl, but she looked so much like Perry that she needed Diana to keep pretending to like her. "His chains. They were too heavy. I didn't think. He was about to fall. So I."

"Vi?"

This time Perry did appear. "How are you feeling?" He stuffed his empty hands into his pockets.

"I'm a little off balanced, but Li's tea has helped to settle my stomach a little."

"I see you've met Diana."

"Of course."

"Yes, I've met Viola. She was just telling me the story of how you met. Something about you not being able to carry your share."

"Shut up Dede."

Diana smirked and exited the kitchen.

Vi climbed the stairs back to Perry's room, with Perry trailing silently behind her.

"Your sister doesn't like me."

"She doesn't like anyone, not even herself. Don't worry about her. I want you to meet my mother."

"No."

Perry looked as if she'd slapped him.

The expression on Perry's face scared her, but she couldn't fight the wave of exhaustion engulfing her. "I don't want to meet your mother. I want to leave."

"You've been here a day. I thought you wanted to know me."

She did, but now she wasn't sure. She needed a family, a place to belong, but could she ever belong to these people? Could the child find a resting place here?

He reached out for her in the same way he'd reached out for her in the library, with the desperation of an unrepentant sinner seeking redemption.

Vi pushed him away without thinking, and a slightly stunned Perry began backing away from her, closing the door behind him. She didn't want him to leave, but his retreating footsteps had already faded. She attempted to follow him anyway, but somehow ended up in Hangman's Hall, mentally tracing Perry's face in each of his ancestors. He had the First's forehead. His nose copied both the Third and the Fifth. The cleft in his chin belonged to the Second. What about his hands? The frames stopped at each ancestor's chest, cutting off the Cannons from their hands into perpetuity. There would be no way to trace the origins of Perry's rough and needy hands. She attempted to recall the Sixth's handshake, but couldn't. She'd been too busy watching him, to feel him. A deep sigh interrupted her failed rememory, and as she turned, Diana stepped out of the shadow.

"Impressed?"

"Of course. This—" Vi waved at the two-dimensional record of Cannon ancestry. "This is a gift."

Diana's eyes never left Vi's face. "Why do you think Mr. Perrion

Cannon the Seventh has chosen you over all those peopled beauty queens
at the University?"

It had been a question Vi asked herself too many times. She answered
the girl in the same way she answered herself each of those times; with a
shrug. She couldn't define the indefinable, at least not with words this girl
might understand. It was a miracle they'd found each other. Maybe their
need had simply been a beacon in the mist. Either way she didn't know,
but even if she did, an explanation would be wasted on Diana.

"Do you think he loves you? For people like us, love is never an
influence. My mother loves the gardener, but she'll never leave this for
him."

Vi remembered the shared space between the woman under the hat
and the gardener trimming nothing. "Money doesn't matter to me."

"Money. The money is mother's." Diana walked closer to Vi. She was
as tall and lean as Perry. Vi found it impossible to hear her and not hear
him. "He really hasn't shared anything with you. Come here peopleless
girl." She pointed at the dead Cannon men. "Look at these faces. This is
the farce we live for."

"It's a blessing to know your people."

Diana laughed. "This is as much of a lie as my virtue, and Perry's
strength of character. He is weak, and I'm a whore. Don't you get it? It's
all a lie, but it only works if we all continue to tell it. They," she pointed
to the dead faces on the wall, "want to be different. They don't want to be
niggers. Whores and cowards maybe, but niggers   never." She turned
toward Vi. "You, peopleless girl, are a nigger." She walked away, leaving
Vi alone in a hall lined with dead Cannons.

Vi walked through the doors, imported from France, making sure
to head in the direction opposite the over-manicured shrubs. Perry's
abandonment; Diana's words; the child's absence and presence; it all kept
her from seeing what was always already in front of her, and she tumbled.

"Are you hurt?"

Vi shook her head no, but the tears she's been holding on to finally
burst through.

Warm arms encircled her, and she leaned into the softness of meaningless sound. The softness covering this mother's heart and the cooing emanating from even deeper, soothed her.

She wiped the snot from her nose. "You must be Mrs. Cannon."

"Please call me Cleo. You must be the one Perry told me so much about."

Perry talked to his mother about her? Perry talked to his mother about her. "I'm sorry. I didn't mean to disturb you. I just needed to take a walk."

Cleo's laugh sounded like church bells, beautiful and ominous. "I've taken many such walks myself. Who was the source of this need? Please don't let it be my dear Perry? Oh yes. My sweet Diana." She walked over to the chair, picked up a half-filled teacup and began to walk back toward the house. "Come child. Li should be opening some cans and adding water to something in preparation for supper by now. We eat promptly at three. "

Vi had no idea how the Cannons' dressed for supper, and Perry couldn't be found, so she chose the same green dress she'd worn to her work-study interview. When she entered the dining room, she realized the dress was two and zero. Both Cleo and Diana wore pastel tank tops and shorts, while Perry had on the jeans and t-shirt from earlier. She attempted to back out of the dining room unnoticed, but of course Diana couldn't let that happen.

"Vi, what a pretty dress. Green is definitely your color. Come, sit next to me."

Vi wanted to refuse Diana's request, but knew her slight would appear unjustified to Cleo and Perry. As soon as she took the proffered seat from Diana, Li began to place dinner on the table. Cleo had not exaggerated in regard to Li's cooking skills. The chicken was the kind busy working mothers picked up from the grocery deli after it had been slow-cooked into a rubbery fibrous effigy of its former self. The watery mashed potatoes were topped with an even runnier gravy. Diana stared at her plate as if her gaze could somehow transform it into something edible.

Vi looked at the empty chair across from Cleo. "Aren't we going to wait for Mr. Cannon?"

"If Daddy is smart, he'll eat at the Club." Diana poured the potatoes onto her plate. "Why exactly did Daddy pay to send Li to that cooking class last winter? At what point will we be seeing any of those recipes?"

"It takes time dear. It all takes time." Cleo seemed to be searching for something on the table. "Li, my ice tea."

When the topped off crystal glass arrived, Cleo lifted it to her lips as if she hadn't tasted anything that refreshing in days.

Though she addressed Cleo, Diana's eyes never left Vi's face. "Just think Mother. If Perry and Viola got married, we would be sisters. I've always wanted a sister. Someone to share all those unshareable things with. Perry was always so closed and quiet, and, well, a boy. But you, you are a real girl aren't you? We could be like sisters, couldn't we Vi." Diana let her fork plop into her potatoes.

Vi had experienced Diana's false warmness before and wouldn't be as easily deceived this time. Vi looked toward Perry's face, but he focused on his mashed potatoes as if he had found a puzzle that needed to be solved. She was alone.

Cleo put her glass down. "It's a shame that you've kept this child hidden from us so long Perry. Why didn't you tell me you were going steady?"

Cleo's use of the word steady to describe any part of what she and Perry shared was almost enough to distract Vi from her admission. Had she been kept hidden?

Perry simply shrugged and went back to moving his food around the plate.

Cleo turned toward Vi. "Viola, do you have any siblings?"

"No. It's just me and my mom."

The warmth traveled to Diana's lovely, plain face. "Are you one of those urban stories? Single working mother, struggling to survive. I bet you're the first in your family to go to college. Isn't that wonderful mother. Vi is such a credit to the race. Do you live in one of those projects that Chicago is so famous for? You know big city poverty is so much more romantic than rural poverty. The country is no shoes or running water, but Chicago. Chicago is gang wars and crack. You should be a writer Vi. You really must write. You must be an example of how one lifts oneself up by one's bootstraps. You must write it down, so those you left behind will know that poverty is a choice, isn't it? Don't you think Mother? Wouldn't that be wonderful?"

A resolved sadness blossomed across Cleo's face that the overflowing crystal could not erase. She sipped her tea, and avoided looking in Vi's direction.

Cleo, like Perry, either couldn't or wouldn't help her. Neither of them could help themselves. She wished for Cecilia Before words. Cecilia wouldn't allow this beautiful plain girl to talk to her like this. She tried to recall, but only visions of Cecilia After's sliced up body came to mind. Vi was truly alone. "Maybe I will write it all down, but right now I think I'm going to excuse myself." Vi pushed back from the table of Cannons and left the dining room.

Perry came into the room just as Vi zipped her suitcase closed. "What's wrong?"

"You keep leaving me alone."

"I was right there."

She leaned against Moby Dick searching for the words to tell him that he'd failed her. "I want to go home."

"Home?"

"Back to school."

"That's not your home, and besides, Mother doesn't want you to leave."

"Perry. Please. Take me home."

Perry's mouth opened before closing firmly. Shaking his head, he moved out of Vi's way and grabbed her suitcase. When she walked out, he followed her out of the door. He placed her bag in silence. Mrs. Cannon stood alone in the shadow of the door's frame.

"Goodbye Mrs. Cannon. Thank you for welcoming me into your home."

"I wish you could stay. Perry told me you have a big exam to study for on Monday." She squeezed Vi's shoulders with both hands.

Vi wanted to fall into her arms, and rest her head where she could no longer rest it on Cecilia. But Cleo stood unsteadily in front of Vi with no real resting place for her own children.

"Are you sure you won't reconsider?" Cleo reached down for the never empty ice tea, and the child suddenly appeared fully formed at her feet.

"Stop!" Vi backed away.

Cleo knocked over the glass, and it shattered against the worn wooden floorboard. The smell of bourbon encompassed them both. Unveiled Cleo stepped back from Vi. "What ghosts are chasing you child?"

The child sat in front of her in the flesh. Was this a sign? If so, what did it signify? "Before out in the garden you said Perry had mentioned me, but at dinner you reprimanded him for keeping me a secret. Which was it?"

"Li! Li!" Cleo's hands were trembling, so she pressed them against the sides of her dress to steady them. "Perry mentions pledging, his classes and graduate school. But I heard something else. Something he didn't talk about. I knew he was keeping something from me. Then you turn up." She looked past Vi, searching through the open door for someone to rescue her. "Li, I need you."

Diana's voice rang out from the other side of the door. "Is everything okay?"

"I'm afraid I've dropped my tea. Please tell Li I've made a mess."

Vi didn't wait for Li, or Diana, or the hungry child to gain footing. She descended the porch and climbed into the car next to Perry.

As they pulled away, Cleo and Diana looked like ghosts rocking on a verandah that only existed in the imaginations of those with short memories. But they weren't her ghosts. They belonged to Perry.

On the way back the crying child sat cradled in Vi's lap. Was she admonishing her for her failure, or applauding her escape? Vi tried to comfort her, replicating the sounds Cleo used to soothe her in the garden. If Perry noticed the soft cooing noises she made the entire way down Hwy 319, he made no comment. Ancestors couldn't be borrowed. Ronnie had gotten it wrong. Legacies couldn't be traded like overused goods at the Swaporama. It was all as simple as biology. The blood couldn't be borrowed. When they reached campus, Vi couldn't find the words to tell Perry the truth; she knew he didn't want her because the one person he claimed to tell everything had never heard of her. He wasn't enough anyway. His bloodlines couldn't save her; the child had stepped out of

203D into the real world. She would have to save herself.

She closed the car door firmly behind her without looking back. If he did say something, Vi couldn't hear him over the hungry screams of the legacy she carried in her arms.

CHAPTER ELEVEN

A staccato silence peppered the buzz and hum of the cicadas. The sounds should have been comforting; a memoriam to the arrival of her second chance, but the walk from the garage to the door proved laborious. Bugs drifted like drunken honeybees in search of their queen, clumsily colliding into anything in their path. The door fell open with no effort, and the panic of the swarming beetles subsided, but as she made her way through the kitchen something felt wrong.

"Vi." The soft cushions of the living room sofa and thick shag carpeting underfoot seemed to absorb the sound of her voice. "Vi." Cecilia's voice grew louder. Was she screaming? Why was she screaming? Was it to hear herself over the dull buzzing of cicadas on the outside or was it from something inside? Vi's bedroom door was closed. A now familiar occurrence in the After. She pushed the door open, but the room stood empty. The sense of dread that began when she stepped through the door seeped into her chest like smoke from a slow-burning fire. She backtracked to the closed bathroom door, pushing against it. It gave way with little effort. Vi lay in the tub with her eyes closed. She looked asleep, except for the blood covering her chest. Cecilia began wiping the blood away, searching for the source. As she wiped, she could feel Vi's strong heart beating beneath her hand. When she washed enough of the blood away, she realized her child didn't complete her task. A ragged bleeding question mark cradled Vi's still intact right breast. She'd cut herself deep, but it would heal. The pain probably saved her.

"Vi wake up. Please. Wake up." Cecilia tried to lift her second chance child, but she was too heavy. She could not do it alone. "Vi, sweetie, you have to wake up. I can't lift you on my own. I need you. Please wake up."

Her eyes fluttered before flying open, exposing a clarity Cecilia hadn't seen in Vi since the age of six, when she'd demanded to know her father's whereabouts. Vi looked down at her chest and the bloody washcloth. "I'm not finished. I have to finish. Cecilia. Please, help me finish."

Cecilia covered Vi's mouth. "You are finished. You are not cutting anything. If I had a spare hand, I would cut a switch and beat you where you lay. Hold the cloth."

Vi didn't move.

In her best don't test me child voice, Cecilia repeated the command. "Hold the cloth."

Vi's hand quickly covered Cecilia's.

"Don't move." Cecilia backed out of the room, praying her child's fear of her was greater than her fear of an imagined cancer. She dialed 911 and instructed the cool-voiced woman on the other end of her location and the nature of her emergency.

CHAPTER TWELVE

"**M**s. Moon. It seems as if your associate is less than on time this afternoon. Please distribute the list today."

Her associate? Not on time? The child sat at her feet as always. Could Dr. Locke see her? Vi opened her mouth to ask just as the realization that he was referring to Tunisia dawned on her. She almost outed herself again. The baby displayed its distress unpredictably, emanating ear-piercing screams like bombs dropping on Beirut. Vi needed something to focus on other than the child's consistent wailing. The only respites came with Ronnie's pills, and she was out. The ghost had turned her best friend into the dope man. A worn cloth-covered book sat undisturbed on Locke's forward desk. It appeared forgotten and alone. Vi didn't fight the urge to touch it. "*The Children of Hercules*?" The child's cry changed pitch. Vi pressed her index finger against the center of her ear.

The movement attracted Locke's attention. "*The Children of Herakles*. It is the story of both great sacrifice and great fear. A Greek tragedy."

Vi looked down again, but the book had disappeared from Locke's desk. The child's screeching intensified. Refocusing on Locke, Vi shook the noise from her head. "Like Sophocles' *Oedipus*."

He stopped in the middle of a purposeful action and turned toward her. His small eyes grew smaller before retracting. "Yes. But this one is authored by my namesake, Euripedes."

Did the parentheses encasing his mouth just soften?

"In order to prevent the children of his enemy, Herakles, from seeking revenge for his crimes against their father, Eurystheus tries to kill them, but King Demophon, no relation to either, is willing to wage war to save them." Dr. Locke sat back in his chair. "That's who this institution is, Eurystheus. We attempt to erase what came before."

"It's not possible. To erase before. Even if Herakles children were killed, they lived, and that historical truth remains unchanged." The wailing deepened as if to emphasize Vi's point. Her past, or more specifically, her mother's past, sat here at her feet, refusing erasure.

"You can't erase lives, but what of the knowledge those lives have gathered? When the body dies, should the knowledge die with it? Somehow we think if we don't agree with it, if it doesn't bolster our own worldview, we have the right to erase it. In the 60's the focus was on the classics, in the 70's it changed to black power, in the 80's we looked back to Africa. And with each wave of the new, everything old ended up on the permanent storage list. Each one, incinerate one."

"But don't we have to make room for new possibilities?" Something in her chest, underneath the keloid question mark twisted. "At some point don't you have to put the past behind you?"

"Ms. Moon you simply can't turn from the truth. It doesn't just go away. If unacknowledged it becomes a shadow, interacting and following. Or it can become something even more intrusive, a monstrous version of its former self, but it is always here." He shook his head and sighed in her direction. "Your world is simply too small and new to comprehend. "

She laughed. Her mother's unacknowledged shadow was here becoming less of a shadow each day. She comprehended. She had no choice, but Locke had already redirected his attention. Vi reached down to grab her backpack from the floor. The child screamed, and the bag fell to the ground. Her latest collected Moon tumbled into view, sliding across the smooth concrete floors. They both stood staring at it as if the tome was a gift from the Gods.

"What's that you have there Ms. Moon?"

She picked it up and held it behind her back with both hands. "Nothing."

"Ms. Moon." He pointed his cloudy eyes toward her.

It was a war of wills she didn't feel equipped to fight, let alone win, so she acquiesced and waved it at him. "A book. Nothing special. Just something I picked up."

"Have you heard nothing. There is no such thing as a book that is not special." Disdain replaced his interest in both her and her book. "But you wouldn't know that. You've never known loss; the loss that proceeds such disregard of context."

She placed the stolen book back into her bag with a certainty she didn't know she possessed. "I know loss." She said it more to herself than to Locke, but he stopped shifting papers and looked at her.

"You do, don't you?" Suddenly he picked up *Herekles Children* and began walking to the back of the warehouse. "Ms. Moon. I hope I'm not wrong about you."

Unsure of how to interpret his reaction, Vi continued to stand in front of his desk, clutching the bag to her chest.

When he noticed her inaction, he stopped and waited for her to follow. Once assured that she was following him, he began walking again. After reaching the outermost limits of the warehouse he pushed aside an empty shelf to reveal a locked door.

Once open, the door revealed a smaller version of the warehouse they just left. Ceiling-high bookshelves stood in front of each wall. Carefully catalogued books lined each bookshelf. "I protect them, even in the midst of threats of war. I will not let them be the victims of revenge or fear. I protect them and catalogue them. I do it because I must. There is no one else to do it. Don't get me wrong Ms. Moon. This is a dangerous endeavor. Eurystheus has a long and deadly reach, but they are worth war, aren't they? And when the world changes again, it will thank me for saving them from themselves."

Vi didn't know what to say or how to react. "It's so quiet."

"Quiet? Can't you hear them? The voices of your ancestors. Listen."

But she couldn't. The child's sudden silence was deafening. Vi trembled.

Locke grinned broadly, attributing her physical reaction to his revelation. "I knew I was right about you? I knew we were like-minded souls."

Were they? Was he as crazy she? Or were they the sane ones?

He guided her back through the door, and she hoped against her rule on hoping the cries wouldn't begin again. As he relocked the door and replaced the bookshelf, he pressed his index finger across his lips. "Remember Ms. Moon. Eurystheus."

Vi nodded, following Locke back to his desk. Vi picked up the list. "Are there any on here that you want me to bring directly to you?"

Locke looked down at the list in her hand and seemed surprised by the whiteness of the page. "One moment Ms. Moon. I seem to have given you one of the administrative copies. I'll take that one." She placed the clean list on his desk, and he handed her a much redder replacement. "Thank you Ms. Moon."

Tunisia busted through the Attic doors still in motion. "Sorry I'm late. My roommate—"

Dr. Locke waved her excuse away with his hand. "You almost missed Ms. Moon. She has the control sheet for the day."

The small window slammed shut, the child began to screech again, and just that quickly her Dr. Locke, the one that had welcomed her into his world, disappeared back into himself. Tunisia's arrival changed everything. So while Locke remained focused on Tunisia's tardiness, Vi picked up the clean list from Locke's desk.

Tunisia frowned. "I thought you were handing out the lists from now on."

He dismissed them both without words and began to rummage through the ledger again.

Vi handed Tunisia the unrevised sheet, and Tunisia snatched it out of her hand without making eye contact. The sheet had barely been touched by Locke's sword. Would she be suspicious of such an uncontrolled control sheet?

"Where you working today? The fourth floor?" Tunisia's toothy presentation bore no warmth.

"No I have Geography today." Vi did not make eye contact. She pushed her cart into the freight elevator.

"Just checking, so I know what spots to avoid, Nasty girl." Tunisia exited the elevator on the first floor.

Any hesitation Vi felt, disappeared. She pushed her cart out onto the third floor. Locke was right. The past shouldn't be left to the whim of short memories and passing trends. It should be recovered and venerated. She pushed the cart through American History three times, making sure she collected every Moon. What if her growing collection of Moon books could be the key to satiating the child's hunger. Perry's name hadn't been enough because the child needed to be fed by her own bloodline. She had to recover as many as she could. It was funny how many Moons appeared once she began to look for them. They were everywhere. Here was a Moon at the center of the Civil War; another appeared in the midst of Manifest Destiny. She circled the Social Sciences, stacking multiple copies of Moon's *Subjects and Citizens* neatly next to *The Last Man on the Moon*. So involved with her search, she didn't hear Tunisia until it was too late.

"What's all that on your cart?"

This girl had the timing of Christopher Columbus, always in the wrong place at the right time. "Books."

"Stop tripping Chicago. We both know that I got Social Science today."

"These? They were   misplaced. I'm reshelving them."

"That's not your job."

"I know, but our lists are so light lately. I figured reshelving is better than hanging out with Locke until the end of my shift." Vi pushed her cart toward the freight elevator, hoping to convince Tunisia of her innocence through action. "I'm going down to Geography now."

Tunisia's expression demonstrated she didn't believe her. "You smell that?"

Vi paused from her performance to witness Tunisia's.

"Smell like fish." Tunisia turned her nose up in Vi's direction and began waving her hand in front of her face. "Just so you know, next time I see unauthorized pulls on your cart, I'm telling Locke." As if to strengthen her threat Tunisia didn't push her cart away until Vi was safely on the freight elevator headed down to Geography.

She'd been careless with her newfound understanding. Her carelessness almost got her caught. Her collection would take time. Locke had been working on his collection for years. But he didn't have to worry about a starving ghost or Tunisia; the Administration, of course, but the majority of the contact he had with the university seemed to be instigated by him. Once Tunisia disappeared from the Social Science section, Vi retrieved the Moons she'd put back. Then the child screamed. Vi turned. Perry.

"Do you hear me?" He took a step forward. "Can you hear me? When I see you, it's like I no longer exist." He took another step forward, placing his foot in front of the cart.

"Perry. I need time." She told the lie to make him go away. She didn't need anything from him or his conflicted history.

"I took you home. You met my family. You said there would never be anything between us. I want it back the way it was. Without words." He grabbed both of her arms and pulled her closer.

She yanked away. "I don't want no words. I don't want —" Over his shoulder, on the shelf to the left. Was that another E. Moon?

"But you   were willing to carry it. You grabbed the chain."

"Perry I don't think I can anymore." She had enough to carry. She couldn't possibly carry his too.

He grabbed her face, pushing his lips against hers. His breath smelled sour, as if he'd swallowed something rotten.

The baby screeched. She moved her head away.

"I disgust you now." He took a step back.

"I have to finish." She stumbled as she pushed the cart away, but kept moving. Tunisia had been witness to Perry's possession of her. She'd been witness and saw only nastiness. Maybe Tunisia was right. Vi had made getting it wrong an art. Perry hadn't been an answer. Perry had only been the source of more confusion. He couldn't offer her a past. He couldn't feed the child. Maybe she should stop Tunisia before she pushed a full cart back down to the Attic. The pop song Tunisia had turned into a damning mantra rang in her ears. Vi's list was shorter than it had been the day before, which had been shorter the day before that. Her control sheet could've been printed on red paper because the white only peeked through. Tunisia's had been almost all white. Vi checked her watch. It would take Tunisia hours to pull all the books on the unedited list, so she decided to secure the Moons she'd collected first. She bagged them in garbage can liners and placed them in the dumpster behind the library to retrieve later. When Vi finally pushed her cart back to the Attic, Tunisia was already standing in front of her book-laden cart beaming with pride.

"You thought you were going to beat me cause you gave me the long list. Check me out. Still pulled faster than your ass." She pushed the cart next to Locke's desk as Vi slid both edited lists on top of Tunisia's unedited copy. When Locke saw the cart overflowing with books, his permanent marker stopped moving. "What is this Ms. Johnson?" He reviewed the list Vi had placed back into his inbox and then back at Tunisia's cart. "You've pulled the opposite of my edits. Who are you working for Ms. Johnson?"

"What? Dr. Locke I work for you. I pulled exactly what was on the control sheet like I always do."

But Dr. Locke had stopped listening. He grabbed book after book from Tunisia's cart, flinging each one to the ground. "Like you always do. Just like you always do. Well I've had enough of this Ms. Johnson."

"Dr. Locke please."

"This is not your first affront to my authority, but it will be your last."

"Without work study, I'm out of school."

"You should've thought of that before you signed on with those fascists in ACPAC."

Vi had seen enough. She exited quietly as the child and its renewed hunger nipped at her heel. Vi headed toward Ronnie and Hughes' Hall without consciously deciding to change her usual path, entering the boys only dorm like she wasn't an interloper, taking the steps to Ronnie's room two at a time. The hall was empty. The door gave way without resistance. Ronnie sat on the bed, looking through a closed window.

"Ronnie. Are you awake? Ronnie?"

"Poorchild is that you?"

"Ronnie I need   ."

"Check in the bottom dresser on the left."

With the pills came a fog. It was just enough to cloud out both sight and sound of the hungry child for at least a little while. It gave her time to think. Previous doubt blossomed into certainty. She didn't need Perry. Perry was only white noise. Tunisia deserved what she'd gotten. And the child? The books would be enough. Hadn't her silence in Locke's room proved that.

"I need you to take a ride with me." It was more of a command, than a request. He climbed off of the bed and walked out the door.

Both his abrupt announcement and action startled her, but she followed him out of his dorm and to his car, grateful to have a distraction.

"No wait. Drive." Ronnie threw the keys in her direction and climbed into the passenger seat.

Blue Thunder roared unevenly under her.

"It's okay. Just don't force her."

Vi pushed the car into third gear. "Where am I taking you?"

"Just take Apalachee Parkway all the way to Capital Circle."

Vi pushed Blue Thunder down the Parkway, away from the library's insanity. She drove until the Albertsons and Ramada Inns disappeared into emptied farmland and bigger than life renderings of future subdivisions.

"Turn into the Circle."

"I hate circles." She turned anyway.

He nodded as if her thoughts were his own.

"Circles always bring you back to the beginning."

Ronnie continued to nod in agreement.

Vi didn't ask what beginning this circle was bringing Ronnie back to.

Ronnie pointed in the direction he wanted her to go.

"You never get to move away from anything without getting closer to it." They entered a newborn subdivision. Each home a replica of the next. Plastic headstones stuck out from identical patches of green lawn and cute ghosts hung from invisible wires. Imposters. All of them. Ghosts were not cute.

"Stop."

At first she thought he meant her discussion on circles. Then she realized he meant the car, so she pressed the brake. Ronnie jumped out of Blue Thunder before she could fully form the question of where and who and disappeared inside of a dark colonial.

Vi was still forming questions when Ronnie returned to the car. There was something so different about the face leaning in the window, but it was an exact replica of Ronnie, so Vi dismissed her altered view. Hadn't she just taken two pills?

"It's going to take a little longer than I thought."

"The thing you're picking up isn't here?"

"Picking up?" He seemed to be searching for an answer. "I never said anything about..."

The face that did and did not belong to Ronnie began to scare her.

"You didn't. I assumed. Don't worry. I'll wait." Did the pills have the power to snatch bodies? No not bodies, souls?

"There's a little buffalo wing spot about a mile up the circle. Just wait there." He handed her a twenty.

This Ronnie didn't want her to wait, and she had no way to ask the other one, so she did as this one asked. Vi drove the car to one of those places that had been really cool the first time it opened, but had lost all of its luster after being thoughtlessly cloned over and over again absent all original context.

Re-imagined cobwebs grew from every corner of the restaurant-bar combination. Plastic eight-legged apparitions threatened to fall from the ceiling onto the bar. Suburbanites filled the tables crowding the center of the restaurant. Vi figured they needed to escape their smaller boxes of repetition, and what better way than collecting in larger clumps at bigger boxes of repetition. Even though Vi didn't know how long it would be before Ronnie would show up, she chose not to wait for a table. The thought of sitting across from an empty chair made something churn inside of her, so she sat at the bar. She had to focus to distinguish the hostess from the bartender, and the bartender from the waitress. Headshots must have been mandatory with each job application. Only faces that could belong to anyone need apply. Only faces that could successfully blow up a federal building or rob a bank and get away with it, need apply.

The possible bank robber tending bar finally noticed her and approached. "Can I get you something?"

She probably shouldn't mix alcohol with the pills she'd already taken, but she needed to extend the silence. "A rum and coke."

The indistinct bartender didn't hesitate or ask for I.D. "Do you want anything off the menu?"

She shook her head, and he plopped the drink down on the bar in front of her.

The rum felt warm and cold sliding down her throat, solidifying her solitude. She was alone for now even if it was both imagined and temporary. No child. No Ronnie. No anyone. For now, but eventually the pills and rum would dissipate from her system, and she would have to go back to only pretending the child didn't exist. She wasn't sure how much longer she would be able to keep it up. Dr. Gabrielle had warned her pretending would only delay the inevitable. Just one more thing the doctor had been right about.

— *What do you want from me?*

— *I want you to be better.*

— *What if I don't get better?*

— *You will.*

— *How will you know?*

— *You'll tell me.*

— *I could just pretend.*

— *To be better? What would that solve?*

— *It would get me out of here.*

— *Then what? If you leave before you're ready, you'll just end up right back here, or somewhere*

— *Somewhere worse?*

— *That's not what I was going to say. I was going to say somewhere different. Somewhere less familiar.*

— *This place is not familiar. I'll have no rememory of here after I leave.*

— *Don't you mean memory?*

— *That's what I said.*

— *No. You said rememory.*

— *Did I? That's funny. I used to call it that when I was little.*

— *Call what?*

— *Someone else's memory.*

—

— *Hasn't anyone ever told you a story so many times it becomes a part of you? And when you retell it it's like you were there. Sometimes you aren't even sure?*

— *My grandfather used to tell me stories like that.*

— *That's rememory. Some of my rememories are more familiar than the memories I make. Cecilia says her stories are my true inheritance. That each generation must remember the last or*

— *Or what?*

—

— *Vi? What happens if you forget?*

— I don't know.   But what I do know is this place   will never be a story I tell.

Even through the drug and alcohol fog, she saw him clearly. Dr. Locke sat alone in a fake web covered booth in the back. But it couldn't possibly be Locke because she'd just left him in the Attic. What would he be doing in a place where buffalos grew tiny wings? But there he sat, she could see him clearly with her own two eyes, and surely that was proof enough. They were her father's after all. Weren't those red fingertips waving at the non-descript waitress? She pushed herself off of the stool and moved toward the waving man with the permanently stained hands. The closer she got to the man the more her clarity retreated, revealing a complete stranger sitting in the booth.

"Can I help you?"

"Where did the other guy go?"

He shook his head. A gold star twinkled from his front tooth. "Sweetie it's just me." He nodded toward the empty space on the other side of the booth. "You want to join me?"

"Where's the other guy with the thick glasses and crazy hair?"

"Sorry sweetie. You're mistaken."

"My name's not sweetie." Vi left him flashing his condescending gold teeth and reclaimed her seat at the bar. Why was she recreating images of Locke? Was he her latest resident apparition? Would that be her life, collecting disconnected souls? She signaled for the bartender to bring her another. She drank that one too fast. Was it crazy to think she could drink herself into normalcy? But even the thought of being crazy disappeared with the third one. She refused a fourth, afraid it would erase this new knowledge of rum and coke's true power.

"Poorchild." Familiarity interrupted her skewed view. Ronnie. "Have you been drinking?"

"Yes." Vi signaled to the bartender to bring her another, her former refusal already dissipating. "Hey you want one for the road?"

"Said the dead girl in the corny after school special." His head leaned to the side. Her Ronnie was back. "I think I better drive back."

Vi hugged him. "How did you get here?"

"I got a ride from a friend."

That's not what she meant. She really wanted to know what had changed him back to himself. She hadn't even thought of a friend, but of course people lived in houses on circles. Of course there was a friend. "Who?"

"Why are you all up in my business?" He spoke with a sharpness usually saved for Others.

Vi physically leaned back from the cut.

Ronnie's face and tone softened. "I can't talk about it. At least not yet. It's not all my business to share."

She wanted to ask when had it not "being his business" ever stopped him, but she nodded and followed him out of the restaurant.

When they got back to campus, Ronnie pulled into Hughes's Hall parking lot, only remembering that Vi's dorm sat on the other side of campus after placing the car in park. She got out of the car anyway, despite his protestations to blame his head not his heart. She needed to walk to clear her head from the alcohol she told him. The old Ronnie would never have let her walk across campus alone and drunk, but this sometimes new Ronnie seemed stuck somewhere deep inside of himself and let her go without a second look back.

She needed to clear her head she told herself. Lincoln's Hall is on the way she told herself. When she walked past the parking lot, she didn't even pretend not to look for Perry's car, but she didn't see it. She tried not to imagine where he could be and who could be riding next to him, but her imagination had never been so easily disengaged. She walked and imagined. She imagined him with the girl that wasn't her. She imagined him at the head of the snake consuming kegs of PBR. She imagined him in Albany at Cleo's feet, nursing falling crocodile tears. She even imagined him waiting for her at the library's dumpster, preparing to share her load of stolen Moons, but when she got there, the books were right where she'd left them, unguarded. She strapped them to her back and headed to Tubman's Towers. Just as Tower D came into view and the sheer weight of her burden began to overwhelm her, the statue at the courtyard's center split in two, and Perry stepped out of her imagination and onto her path

He watched her struggle forward with an expression she couldn't read. When they stood face to face, he lifted his shirt. "It's healed. Touch it."

Vi didn't want to touch it, but she did. The Gamma interlaced with the Nu stood out against his smooth flesh. Surprisingly, it felt soft against her fingers. It's violent appearance suggested hardness.

"My father called me the other day." He let the shirt fall. "He reprimanded me."

"For what?"

"For you. For bringing you home with me."

" For me?" Vi swayed under the weight of the Moons in her backpack. "What am I supposed to do with that?"

"I'm trying to understand what's wrong with you?"

"Everything is wrong with me. Can't you see that? I'm different."

"From them?"

She shook her head. "From you."

"But we're different together."

"That doesn't make us the same."

Perry's voice became higher and louder. "But our difference marks us as the same."

Vi was confused. He was wrong, wasn't he? It had made sense. It had been clearer, if not clear. Now she wasn't sure. She turned away from him unsteadily, attempting to gain her balance.

"If you walk away from me this time, this is it."

She continued toward the door.

"If you won't see me, I won't see you. Do you understand Vi? I won't see you."

She hesitated a fraction of a second before disappearing into Tubman's Tower D.

Even though she hadn't seen or talked to Ronnie since that mysterious drive out to Capitol Circle, he looked like he belonged there, in her room, sharing her space. She was glad that he'd stopped by after class.

"So Poorchild have you decided what you are going to be for Halloween?" He sat cross-legged on Danielle's old bed, filling up the empty side of 203D without artifice or effort; unaware of the hundreds of

Moons and baby hidden underneath it.

"Myself." She could think of nothing scarier.

He laughed. "Now that was funny. But there must be something that you've always wanted to pretend to be. How about Superwoman? No you need someone blacker. What about Kitt's Catwoman, or the Almighty Isis, the historically-correct version of course."

Vi couldn't be a superhero. She couldn't get through the day without pills and a caterwauling ghost. Ronnie was the closet thing to a superhero she'd known, accept of course for Cecilia Before. "What about you?"

He flipped through her closet. "Maybe I'll be you."

"Why would you want to be me?"

"That's it. Let's switch." He grabbed the green dress from the back of the closet. "You could be me, and I could be you."

"I can't be you." Vi wished she could be Ronnie. He was so sure, even when he wasn't. She exhausted her pretending muscle completing the most mundane daily activities.

He waved her doubts away with one hand, as he placed the dress in front of him with the other. "Of course you can. Remember? I am you and you are me."

She didn't have the heart to tell him his ancestors hadn't stood the test of time. That she and he were as separate as Booker T.'s five fingers, so she went along with it. She let him take her green dress, and listened as he coordinated what he'd christened the largest act of revolution A&M had seen in years.

A collective gasp escaped when the girl walked into the classroom. It took Vi a moment to realize exactly who had forced the class toward a joint anything. She was pretty, but her beauty grew out of something less glossy. Vi recognized her own green dress as the girl moved toward her with a look of familiar surprise.

"Where's your Ronnie suit?" For the first time since she'd met Ronnie, she saw uncertainty flash across his face.

She shrugged. She should've warned him, but she knew he would've talked her into it. "Sorry."

The tittering around them only grew louder.

"Always knew Old boy was a faggot."

Neither one of them turned. The voice didn't need a face. His words were enough.

Dr. Bennett finally interrupted once the class responded to the voice with unbridled laughter.

With a look that Vi couldn't read, Dr. Bennett motioned the class into silence. "Relax class. It's just a joke. Lets get down to business."

"A joke?" Ronnie whispered it to himself, but his discomfort reverberated through Vi.

"This is the perfect opportunity to readdress our conversation about the willful destruction of the Black Male psyche. Is this," he gestured toward Ronnie in Vi's dress, "a sign?"

"Of course it is." It was the same voice from before. "They dress us all up and call it comedy. They did it to Flip Wilson first. Then Eddie Murphy and Martin Lawrence. But it's not funny. It's public castration."

Another voice interrupted. "Damn Man. Are you saying old boy doesn't have any thing swinging under that dress?"

Laughter permeated from every corner of the classroom, including Dr. Bennett.

Ronnie stood up. "What does it mean to be a black man?"

Dr. Bennett looked around as if Ronnie couldn't be addressing him.

Ronnie did not sit down. "What does it mean to be a black man in America?"

Dr. Bennett waved Ronnie back into his seat. "A man is a man. A woman is a woman. It's physiology. It's biological. It's not up for question. Do I need to review how you tell the difference?" There was a dare in his question, that the class answered with more teetering laughter.

"I am a man." He moved to the front of the class. "In a dress or out of one. You know that better than most; don't you Marcus?" Ronnie reached under Vi's dress and grabbed his groin. "Or do you need a review of last night?"

The teetering stopped.

Both of Dr. Bennett's faces visibly fell. "You need to leave."

Ronnie's anger overflowed onto his cheeks. "I'm already gone." As Ronnie walked out the door, he paused and turned back toward Vi. A second chance? He was giving her another chance at redemption. He waited for her, but instead of finally being the friend he had been to her, she found a spot of smudged chalk on the board and concentrated on it. They were not one. They were different. He could take that dress off. Ronnie was strong in ways she could never be. By the time she was able to look at Ronnie, the space he occupied was empty. Dr. Bennett remained in front of the lecture hall with both faces revealed. It was as if all the weight of carrying both selves had aged him a decade in a moment. His transformation reminded her of Cecilia Before and After. This was Dr. Bennett After. Would he be one or two? Would this help him reconcile himself with himself? Vi and the rest of the class simply watched in silence as Dr. Bennett, unable to bear the weight of both selves, left the classroom.

After fortifying herself with two more pills, Vi headed to Ronnie's room. When she arrived, Ronnie, still in her dress, stood in the mirror surveying himself from all sides. His full smile contradicted his swollen eyes. "I showed him, didn't I Poorchild? He didn't see that coming, did he?"

She sat at his desk, afraid to cross the space suddenly between them. "Why did you say those things?"

He turned toward her with a look of incredulousness. "Are you blind to everything but your own shit?" He stripped off her dress, and stood in his boxers and eyeliner. "You're so busy chasing that frat boy all over campus that you can't see what's right in front of your face. That nigger don't want you. Have you ever been on a real date? Has he introduced you to any of his frat brothers? He sneaks into your dorm room in the middle of the night and fucks you. And you let him. That's not love. Trust me Vi. I know what I'm talking about."

"He took me home."

"What?"

"He took me home to Albany. To spend the weekend with his family." Vi didn't tell the rest, only the piece that proved she wasn't always wrong.

"Shit." Ronnie slid to the floor. "I've been calling you Poorchild, and who was the one truly getting fucked."

She understood now. She understood the old and new Ronnie. She

understood the circle. She understood the dress. Dr. Bennett was the
friend. He was the one that had almost split Ronnie into two, like Cecilia's
disease, but he hadn't. Ronnie was still here. Vi pulled him to his feet.
"Change and let's go."

"Vi it's too late. "

It wasn't. He'd saved her, and she'd let him walk out alone, but she
wouldn't leave him again. She pushed and pulled until he was settled in
Blue Thunder's passenger seat. She didn't know how she found her way
back into the middle of nowhere, but she turned onto Ronnie's family's
land without any direction from him.

"Stop the car."

"But the red oak is still…"

"Stop I want to see my mother."

"But Ronnie."

"Stop the goddamn car Vi."

Vi guided Blue Thunder into the front yard of the small clapboard
house. The sun hung low in the sky, but the sweltering temperature had
yet to follow suit. Sweat ran down every part of Vi in a futile defense to
the heat. Ronnie leaned over to the driver's side and rammed the pinto's
high-pitched horn without warning. He pushed on the horn again longer
and harder. Climbing on top of the car, he screamed at the house. "Crazy
Mary! Your baby's home." The pinto's roof buckled like an aluminum can
in response to each step. "Come on out and see what you made. Mary. I
know you're in there. Come out and face your creation."

The house remained still.

Vi climbed onto the roof alongside Ronnie. The roof sizzled as her
damp skin made contact. Blue Thunder groaned under their combined
weight. She pulled him down to sit next to her. "What happened?"

"She didn't want me. I was ten when she left and never came back to
get me. Daddy said she wasn't right in the head and leaving me was the
best thing she could've done. But I know it's because I was the way I am.
She didn't want me because I'm a fag."

She stared at the white house, wondering what magic lay just on the
other side of the worn threshold. Did Crazy Mary have the power to wash
away Ronnie's sins and make him whole? Did blood truly wield that type

of power? She wasn't sure, but the fragile world she'd managed to build here was melting around her, and she couldn't just watch Ronnie split into two like Cecilia, so she imagined what Cecilia Before would've done.

"Enough Ronnie. It's too hot for this shit. Get your ass in the car."

Surprisingly he did what she said without argument. She drove them both to the cemetery, drug him to the foot of the red oak, and pushed him to his knees at the bottom of the tree. "What do you want Ronnie? Ask them."

He shook his head back and forth, refusing.

"Ask them. Ask them for what you want. They'll give it to you. They belong to you." She tried to force his open palms together, but instead he moved his open hand across her cheek, wiping away the sweat sprouting from every pore. He moved his hand from one side of her face to the next. As his palm grazed her mouth, Vi grabbed it with both of her hands and held it against her lips. Then she kissed him.

He resisted only for a moment before kissing her back. He found the raised question mark around her breasts. "It's half a heart." He kissed it, and she let him. She had always thought of her scar as a sign of a thing unfinished; a question without an answer, but a heart? Before either of them was sure of what they were doing, he was inside of her. They didn't speak during or after.

They rode back to her dorm in silence, and Vi had the car door open before she had the courage to break it. "Did you ask them for anything?"

He kept his eyes pointed toward the windshield. "Happiness. I asked to be happy."

She leaned in to give him a kiss, but he barely offered her his cheek.

It was late, but there was one witness to her walk of shame. He wore a t-shirt and sweatpants. His short hair formed an unkempt carpet across the top of his head.

He stood in front of her, a wall of flesh and blood and legacy and unforgiveness.

"Perry." She tried to walk around him, but he matched her every attempt to pass with his own attempt to keep her there.

"I am Perrion Cannon the Seventh."

"I know. Have you been drinking?"

"You cannot simply walk away. You prefer that fag to me?" He moved closer before stepping back in disgust. "You stink."

"You're drunk."

"Did you fuck him?   Diana was right. You're just a nigger."

"I am what you are. We're the same. Remember."

"We're not the same. We're from two different places."

"But we're both here now. In this place and neither one of us is a nigger."

"You said you would help me carry it. You are a liar and a nigger." He pushed her, and she fell. He climbed on top of her, looked past her face and rammed himself inside of her. She clawed at him, his face, his eyes, his chest, his arms, but he was a wall. She started to scream, but then the thought of someone coming and seeing what Perry was doing to her. The shame. So she didn't. When he was done and gone, she continued to lay at Harriet's sandaled bronze feet, praying for rain to fall and wash away what Perry had done. But her prayers, as usual, weren't answered, and she carried what he rammed inside of her back up to 203D.

CHAPTER THIRTEEN

At the Centre, dewy magnolias buttressed by windblown cattails blossomed on every wall. Cecilia allowed the magnolias to lead her to her child. Cecilia didn't know what she expected; Vi in a tiny twin bed, covered in white blankets with tubes flowing into a beeping machine. But when she pushed opened the door, Vi sat tucked into an over-stuffed armchair, looking out of a window lined with curtains that matched the magnolia-covered bedspread; her knees pulled up to her chest with pink fluffy footies poking out as if legs without thighs. She could've been watching a movie in the family room or taking a study break in her bedroom. She looked like herself before. Cecilia had to consciously adjust her subconscious expectations. This wasn't that kind of hospital. Vi wasn't that kind of sick. Tubes and beeping machines couldn't fix this. Vi's illness couldn't be cut away no matter how sharp the knife.

Vi turned toward her and smiled.

Cecilia wanted to gather her up into her arms, but stopped, afraid to disturb the literal rupture that Vi had cut between them. Had it healed? Would a hug hurt? Instead Cecilia sat in the chair in front of the window, directly opposite from Vi. "How are you feeling?"

"Fine. I feel really fine."

"You look like.   You look like yourself."

The corners of Vi's mouth quivered. "I never stopped being me."

"Do you want me to bring anything from home?"

Vi looked up, surprised. "Why would you need to do that? I'm leaving here soon."

"Let's not rush things. Dr. Gabrielle doesn't want you to leave before you're really ready."

"I was really ready to leave a week before I got here." Vi unfolded herself from the easy chair and kneeled in front of Cecilia with glistening eyes. "I won't try to hurt myself. I promise. I know that I don't have breast cancer. I realize that your cancer isn't my cancer."

"It's my fault isn't it? I should've talked about it. I should've paid more attention. Maybe counseling." She watched to see if Vi understood. She needed Vi to know not to blame herself. Cecilia remembered a time when words were useless between them because understanding lived beyond sound, but cancer changed that, and she didn't know how to get it back. She hadn't tried hard enough, but she didn't know how to apologize to Vi in a way she would understand or twist her words into something they weren't, so Cecilia abandoned words and pulled Vi up off her knees, gathering her onto her lap, like she should've done the moment she entered the room. She rocked her child—her only child, slow and steady until Vi relaxed, like she used to—against breasts that were no longer there.

CHAPTER FOURTEEN

The next morning cramps pulsated through her abdomen; her uterus attempting to expel the thing Perry pushed into her. She spent the whole morning in a bathroom stall, but the thing remained, stuck. What did Perry ram inside of her? His fear? His anger? Maybe his powerlessness? She didn't know, but she knew she didn't want it, that it didn't belong to her. Eventually the cramps subsided enough, and she was able to go to work.

The Attic was dark except for the halogen lamp that had until now sat unilluminated on top of Dr. Locke's desk. For the first time Vi felt as if she stood in an actual subbasement. The lone lamp exposed a truth Locke's bright fluorescent lights had hidden. The irony of clarity absent light wasn't lost on her. Dr. Locke stabbed the numbers on the phone's keypad with a ferocity usually saved for his crimson marker. She entered the small circle of light illuminating his desk just as he slammed the phone back into its cradle.

"Ms. Moon, good of you to show up. It would be moot for me to question your unexcused tardiness at this juncture." Stacks of red paper covered his usually meticulous desk, giving his workspace the appearance of a murder scene. "Ms. Moon there is no time to waste." He scooped up a random sampling from the pile.

She hesitated before accepting them from Dr. Locke's outstretched hand. The absence of the light made the papers appear even more blood-soaked.

"We must try to catch up." His unfocused eyes moved back toward the phone.

Vi stood stuck to the floor. As stuck as the thing Perry had put into her. She stared at Locke's trembling hand, unwilling to participate in his descent.

Locke's head moved in Vi's direction without actually completing the turn. "Are you interested in joining Ms. Johnson?"

In response she accepted the list from his unsteady grasp and collected her cart, determined to push Locke's deterioration to the edges of her consciousness. She had to focus on herself. She realized her only chance to be whole was through her Moons. The pills were only a temporary fix, keeping the child at bay at least during the day, but the child continued to visit her at night, disappearing at dawn. Each time taking a bit more of Vi's sanity, each time leaving a little less of her in the real world. The drugs couldn't keep the baby away. Vi's only path back had to be through her legacy, her familial name. The answer lived somewhere in one of her books. She shook her trepidation about Locke's mental state away. The shorter Locke's list, the more time she had to expand her own list.

Locke turned his attention back toward the phone. "I don't have the time for this. Why aren't they answering my calls? Has that printer slowed?" The printer's clicking and buzzing seemed to grow louder and faster as if to punctuate Dr. Locke's rhetorical rant. He held the receiver to his ear, waited for a few seconds, and then hung up, only to repeat the process. "There will simply never be enough time."

Vi pushed her empty cart onto the third floor without even referring to Locke's truncated list— the white barely viewable. She could collect her books without fear of discovery. She'd gotten Tunisia fired. At least she succeeded at something. Why didn't she feel more jubilant? She stopped in Astrology. As of late, she'd been forced to leave earth to find evidence of her legacy. There were almost too many Moons to choose from once one was willing to leave the planet. She no longer discriminated regarding authorship. A moon in the title, in a picture, or anywhere, qualified a text to be moved onto her cart. As she stacked three new Moons onto her cart, the child appeared mouth agape. Instinctively, Vi closed her eyes. When she opened them again, the child was gone, but several students peppered the astrological section in small but consistent clumps. The clumps were worse for Vi, like grenades with hypersensitive safeties, ready to disengage with the slightest jostle. And a crazy girl stealing books and seeing ghosts, definitely jostled. Humming to distract herself from any sudden reappearances of the child, she pushed the cart away from the more populated area. A muffled sob interrupted Vi's contemplation of alternative routes through the stacks, so she concentrated to isolate the real from the imagined. Vi moved toward the sobs stiffly. She almost stumbled over it, or more specifically, her; Danielle appeared crouched in a study cublicle cluttered with open books and marked-up pages. While Vi was surprised by Danielle's sudden appearance, Danielle's sobs were less surprising. Anyone with that much external joy had to be suppressing generations of hurt. Vi rested her hand on Danielle's shoulder and, in the way that human contact almost always does, the external walls gave way to the instinctual as Danielle leaned into Vi's embrace. Vi understood hiding in dark small spaces to suffer in silence, but to know Danielle shared her practice gave her comfort. She missed Danielle and her room-filling noise. But their sudden reunion was cut short by the sound of several pairs of high-heeled pumps clicking against the worn tile. Danielle's line sisters. Just as quickly as Danielle had leaned into Vi's arms, she pulled away and stood up, returning the chaos in the cubby to orderly stacks and placing them back into her book-bag. It transpired so efficiently that it must've been performed with regularity. The line of girls in black formed a wall between them. Danielle momentarily disappeared, reappearing in line, number four from the front. As the line moved forward, Danielle stumbled over something that Vi couldn't see, but before Vi could step forward to help, the girls both behind and in front, reached out and steadied her. Watching them move away as a unit, Vi knew Danielle would always be the one on line, and she would always be the one off line. But Vi was doing something to change that. Her books would change that. After filling up her cart, she bagged her latest pulls and placed them in the dumpster. Vi pushed the empty cart through Social Sciences into Early World History and back to the Attic, pulling the few books Locke had left unaltered on the Control Sheet. Locke remained at his desk punching numbers on the phone. But now his screams stood in the stead of silence between the punching and hanging up.

"Dr. Shamus, This is not my first message as you are probably aware. I am under extreme pressure here, and I need to meet with you as soon as possible. You must understand the part that the Attucks Collection plays in the cultural development of this campus. You can not keep clearing the shelves of the classics for this new wave of afro-nationalist rhetoric. Please call me as soon as possible to set up a meeting." He slammed down the handset and looked wide-eyed at Vi's cart. "What have you done?"

Vi assessed the books in her cart. None of her Moons were mixed in.

"What have you done? How could you have removed these?"

"They were on the Control sheet."

"Impossible." He grabbed the crumpled sheets from her outstretched hand. "This is not possible." He scanned the papers through his thick glasses. "How did I miss these? Why would they mark *Parmenides* and *Heraclitus* for removal? This is not possible. This is simply not possible." He fell into his chair, collapsing in on himself, like a half-filled balloon pricked by a pin.

"Why don't you just put them in the room?"

"Do you think it's that simple? Move them into a room. A room with finite walls and shelves. What happens Ms. Moon when those shelves are filled? What happens when I am no longer here to guard them? What happens then?" White foamy saliva collected in the corners of his mouth

Vi stood in silence, afraid her words might make it worse.

"Do you understand? No you don't see. I was right before. Go. Go and live your life. Paint your toenails. Giggle over boys, drink until you pass out. Go do whatever you do outside of here. Go and live your little life unaware. I'll stay here and mind a world on the verge of cultural self-destruction."

Vi backed out of Locke's circle of light, not feeling comfortable enough to take her eyes off of him. Once out of the library, she pushed Locke's madness from her mind. She was not like Locke. She unsuccessfully tried to retrieve her Moons from behind the library, but there were too many to carry alone. She was not like Locke. They were not the same. She would have to return for the rest later.

She stood in the center; the courtyard where everything met. If you went south you would be in King's Dining Hall, West to Woodson's library, East to Tubman's Towers, North to Lincoln's Hall. This was the core of Vi's universe. A girl with white wires hanging from each ear bumped into her. The wires twisted with the girl's head when she turned to glare at Vi. A warning. Watch where you walk. Be careful who you come into contact with. A warning Vi heeded her entire life, until Perry. Her arm throbbed from the contact. These people were real. The child was not. The child was real. These people were not. She stopped moving. He came straight toward her, but he didn't see her. He was real. She was real. The child was real. Or were they all imagined? Shouldn't she be somewhere? Shouldn't she be rushing to reread, restudy, and rewitness something someone else had read or studied or witnessed? Why was she out here in the Center waiting for him and pretending she wasn't? As he approached, she noticed a look on his face she couldn't recall from their time before. Could it be shame? Complicity? Did he know what he did to her? She didn't move, placing her self in his direct path, just like she did that day before today. That day when he and his fraternity moved her. Today she wouldn't be moved. He drew nearer, but his eyes never found her face, even when she stood close enough to smell the cologne his sister gave him for his birthday. Just as collision was inevitable, he stepped slightly to the right. He lied. That thing he did to her, the way he pushed himself inside of her without her permission, without her willingness, without her want, had not rendered her unseeable. He saw her. She watched his back as he retreated, untouched, but moved. Then the pain he pushed inside of her began to claw its way up from between her thighs, past her womb into her pounding chest. The pounding sat at the back of her throat burning. She clamped her hand over her mouth before running from A&M's Center and puking behind a thicket of bushes. The ground soaked it up quickly. By the time she wiped the crevices of her mouth clean, nothing more than a slightly darkened stain remained in the dirt. With nowhere else to go, she fell back in line with everyone else on campus and headed to class.

The air in Sociology felt thick. More students sat in class than had been since the beginning of the semester. Ronnie in her dress. It seemed like a lifetime. Under the red oak. She didn't want to remember the stone wall between them. Her calls remained unanswered, and she didn't have the courage to stake out his dorm. Still, she held onto the hope that whatever had grown up between them in the graveyard would disappear, unlike the rumors left behind from his run-in with Dr. Bennett. Had you heard that Ronnie Tredway had given Dr. Bennett The Aids, and then had the nerve to go to his house and tear up his tests result in front of his wife and kids? Had you heard that Ronnie Tredway was a woman masquerading as a man and had been having an affair with Dr. Bennett? Had you heard that Dr. Bennett had raped Ronnie Tredway and he was going to press charges and sue the University? He's going to get paid. The whispered and not-so whispered rumors no longer followed her. It was all about Ronnie now. She waited for Dr. Bennett to appear with everyone else, wondering how Dr. Bennett would counter the attacks.

When a woman with a fiery auburn head of frizzy hair and clear blue eyes entered the lecture hall the buzzing grew into a roar. "Hello I'm Dr. Schlater. Dr. Bennett has taken a leave of absence and will not be returning this semester."

"I heard he got The AIDS."

"Please. There's no need to speculate on why Dr. Bennett is unable to continue. His leave is due to personal issues, meaning they're not up for discussion. All you need to know is that your credits are safe. Now let's talk about the African familial structure."

Vi stopped listening after that. Dr. Bennett had run off. Ronnie's revelation had forced a man's displacement. Would moving change Dr. Bennett? Is place that significant? Had it mattered for her? She carried her legacy in her blood. Did that mean she couldn't outrun it? How does one outrun something as essential as blood? Was Dr. Bennett's dichotomy blood-based? Will he be able to integrate both of his faces into one or will he simply be dragging both selves into a new classroom on a new campus? And would either face mourn the loss of Ronnie? It was the first time she considered it. If Dr. Bennett loved Ronnie then surely Ronnie, the whole and complete Ronnie, could love Dr. Bennett. She shouldn't have left him alone. She should've stayed with him last night. She ran to Hughes' Hall after class. Maybe hearing he ultimately won would be enough to bury what had come between them in the graveyard.

She knocked. No answer. She knocked again and the door swung open.

The room was a single. Instead of pushing the twin to the wall,

Ronnie had placed his bed in the center of the room, separating the desk from the dresser.

Ronnie stood at his desk, putting books into a box. He looked up at her as if he expected her, but he didn't stop packing. "If you've come for the happy pills, they're over there." He gestured toward the dresser.

Not knowing what to do with herself, Vi followed his nod and leaned up against the dresser. A generation of bumper stickers lined the top like paint. SAY NO TO DRUGS barely covered WHERE'S THE BEEF?

He taped up another box. "I'm done altering my consciousness. They're yours. Take them. Sell them. Flush them. It's up to you."

"Why are you packing?"

He didn't answer.

"Ronnie?" She wanted to put her arms around him and make him stop folding, but the bed blocked her.

"I'm leaving. This place is no longer for me."

"But you don't have to leave. Haven't you heard? Dr. Bennett left. You won."

Ronnie shook his head and continued packing.

"But what about the revolution?"

"The revolution?" He chuckled half-heartedly. "There was never any revolution. Only me not willing to stand in my truth." He extended his hand across the bed.

She took it.

"These foolish boys who think playing with their own dicks make them fags want me dead. They think if I'm gone then they can somehow kill that part of themselves."

Vi opened her mouth, but Ronnie silenced her.

"They don't realize that we aren't the same. That I'm not them. And even if I die, it will still be in them. Guess I'm not much of a revolutionary. Turns out I'm not willing to die for someone else's understanding."

"But   how can you just walk away."

"I'm not walking. Poorchild I'm running. I'm going to go to Miami or Atlanta. Somewhere black men can love black men out in the open and in full color. I'm not built to hide. Yes, I've decided that I'm gay. That I will love only men."

"Place won't change anything." Didn't she know that more than anyone? There was nowhere to run. Her dress lay across the stripped bed like any other unexceptional collection of fabric and thread with its true power cloaked by the dry cleaner's thin plastic covering. Is that what Superman's cape looked like between uses? "I think you should keep it."

"No, that belongs to you. I was only borrowing it.   Besides it's infamous now."

Vi clutched the dress to her chest, hoping that it possessed some fragment of Ronnie Before.

"Hey. I want you to have something else." He handed her a blue and white tie-dyed rabbit's foot with a key attached.

"Blue Thunder?"

"Where I'm going Blue Thunder can't take me. Take her."

She couldn't watch as Ronnie continued to pack himself in boxes and prepare to leave her. She walked out with her infamous dress in one hand and a rabbit's foot and baggie full of pills in the other, and she was almost alone.

CHAPTER FIFTEEN

The doctor exiting the Magnolia suite looked young enough to be Vi's older sister. Cecilia worried that she should've asked for someone older with more experience. What could this barely a woman tell her about her child she didn't already know?

The doctor patted Cecilia's shoulder reassuringly as if anticipating her doubts. "Mrs. Moon, I expect to see Vi back here at least once a week until she leaves for school."

"Dr. Gabrielle. Is she?"

"Ready? Of course."

Had she found the thing the other doctors had not been able to find? Had she managed to exorcise the demon that Vi tried to self-excise. Cecilia wasn't sure. "But to go so far away from home."

"Vi needs this. She needs space."

"From what? Me? She needs to be away from me? So that's your prognosis?"

"No. Not you. But she does need space to develop her own sense of self absent you. Though she understands you are a separate person, on some very basic level she believed that you and her were the same person."

"Is it something I did?"

"There's no need to place blame. Children love their parents. For some children that love can become something else. She was unable to see a future for herself separate from yours. She saw it as some sort of genetic legacy. So when you were diagnosed with breast cancer…"

"She thought she would be." Why had she not seen this? She spent so much of her time making sure her premonition didn't become reality that she created a reality that almost yielded the same results.

The magnolia suite door opened, and Vi walked out to meet them.

Cecilia examined her for difference, but she could find nothing. She didn't look sick. The scars she'd carved into her chest were safely covered by the A&M sweatshirt Cecilia had just given her as both a Coming Home and Going Away present.

"Are you ready?" The words didn't capture her full meaning, but Cecilia watched Vi for a sign she understood the question anyway.

Vi nodded, waved at Dr. Gabrielle and started toward the exit. Cecilia, still unsure if Vi fully understood the question, followed Vi onto the elevator and out into the parking lot anyway. Vi stood with her face up to the sun, waiting for Cecilia to open the trunk.

"You need help with that?"

"Nope. I got it."

Cecilia watched from the curb, as Vi loaded her bag into the trunk and climbed into the car without one look back at either the Centre or her mother.

CHAPTER SIXTEEN

When she reentered the Attic, Dr. Locke's absence echoed through the cavernous space. A heavy-set woman with glasses perched on her forehead sat behind his desk.

"What happened to Dr. Locke?"

She pulled the glasses down over her eyes and looked Vi up and down. "The thing that always happens to Dr. Locke."

"Is he coming back?"

"He always does. Tenure is a wonderful thing." An opened newspaper sat in front of her on Locke's desk. "I'm Mrs. Lattimore. I'll be running long-term storage temporarily. Here's your list."

Vi reached forward and stumbled. There was something more than Locke missing; the Attic's heartbeat. "Why isn't the printer running?"

"That old thing. Why would it be?" She peered over her glasses.

"When Dr. Locke is here, the printer never stops."

"Sweetie, I'm not sure what you're talking about, but there is no one on the other side of that old thing. The pull list is generated monthly and distributed through email. They actually bring down Locke's copy because he refuses to use a computer."

How could that be? How many times did she watch Locke pull reports from that printer? How many times? Vi started to tell her about the revisions, but Mrs. Lattimore, with her over the reading glasses eyes, didn't appear to value revision. Vi never imagined actually missing the sound of the dot matrix printer moving back and forth across the roll, but she did. She also never imagined seeing Tunisia in the Attic again, but here she was, behind a cart, waiting in front of the freight elevator, just like before. "Dr. Locke talked about you like you were dead."

"Yeah. That old nut thought I was working for the Administration. It don't matter though cause he wasn't never really running stuff no way.

After he fired me, Dr. Cristabel figured he was really losing it and decided it was time to step in again."

So Vi had gotten it wrong again. She had not been the source of Tunisia's dismissal, but had she been the source of Locke's vacation?

"You know, Frenchtown Gardens. Dr. Locke got him a permanent suite down there."

"What?"

"Girl, where you been? You ain't heard about Old Dr. Locke. He used to run this place."

"The library?"

"No Chicago, The whole University. They say he lost it back in the nineties. Went to a Kwanzaa celebration in full Greek toga. No drawers or nothing. They say the family jewels was on display and everything. That was the first time they sent him over to Frenchtown Gardens. After that, seem like he'd get better, just to go back every other year or so."

How had Dr. Locke descended to the Attic from the Head of the University? If a man as erudite as Locke couldn't figure out how to survive without pretending, what hope did she have? "The printer. What about the printer?"

"What printer? Shoot. I need me a job I can't get fired from, even if I show up at work butt-naked. Right, Chicago?"

Vi nodded in agreement, but she wanted Tunisia to stop talking. The next time she needed to get rid of someone, she would be sure to come up with a more permanent plan.

And just like that Tunisia seemed to wipe Locke from her conscious view. "You going home for the break?"

Home was a foreign concept. Return was not possible. "No money. I'm going to stay in the dorm." How could Dr. Locke be erased from this place so easily and quickly?

"You mean you going to HAH?"

"What?"

"They close the dorms over the break. If you're not going home, you staying at H.A.H., Home Away from Home Rec Center, but it's just a piece of shit camp at the edge of town they ship all the homeless dorm residents to. They couldn't pay me to stay there."

Vi shrugged the idea of further displacement away, still stuck on Tunisia's denial of the printer and erasure of Locke. How had she shared in his delusion so completely?

They were still in front of the freight elevator. Mrs. Lattimore now sat behind a magazine with a woman with blowing hair across the cover, and expressed no concern over the non-movement of their carts. Vi needed to escape all the difference that Locke's banishment had fostered, so she made a request that she would've never asked of Locke. "Mrs. Lattimore, do you mind if I leave early? I have a paper to turn in."

Mrs. Lattimore barely looked over her glasses this time. "Of course dear. This place pretty much takes care of itself. Enjoy your break."

On the way back to Tubman's Tower the thick humid air helped to keep Vi on her feet. Was she truly insane like Locke? His ghost printer and her ghost baby, both fortified by books that the world had forgotten. What about Perry? Wasn't what he did crazy? Where was the line that separated his crazy from her crazy? Sometimes she found herself looking for him in strange places, but when she found him he still pretended not to see her. Is it crazier to see someone who doesn't exist or to not see someone who does? Maybe she could use Perry's method and write it down; record it as a way to release it. Back in her room, she put her pen to paper and let it move, but when she read it back, she realized she'd only written the word crazy over and over again.

— *What makes me crazy?*

— *Vi no one is saying you're crazy.*

— *Is that why people come to the Centre? Because no one says they're crazy.*

— *People come here for a lot of reasons. Some come for a much needed respite. Others come because they have things they need to work out. Others come*

— *I tried to give myself a mastectomy. Where do I fit?*

— *You don't need to fit Vi.*

— *I don't fit that's why I'm here. I had the nerve to disagree with the diagnosis, so that makes me crazy.*

— *Not crazy. Vi I'm more interested in why you believe you have cancer.*

— *Is the why more important? If I have it, would the why be more important?*

— *But all your tests were negative. Your doctors believe*

— *So my sanity is not about my why, it's about my belief versus the doctor's belief*

— Do you believe in God?

—

— Do you?
— Yes
— Can you prove God exists?
— No, but I have faith.
— You believe in a man in the sky that controls and assists everyone and everything. At least the good sound stuff. Because everything bad is blamed on his shadowy nemesis. Right?

—

— Yet you are sane and I'm not.
— But Vi this isn't about my belief.
— It is. Because you have the power to keep me here. I am crazy because I and only I believe I have a cancer that will eventually destroy me.

—

— But what you need to know is I will never again try to cut it away. I know the cutting will kill me now, and the whole point of all of this was to live. Do you understand? I know even if you don't, and that has to be enough. Do you understand?
— Yes. Vi. I understand

Her difference didn't make her crazy. The cutting did. As long as she didn't hurt herself, she would be okay. Hearing things that weren't there was okay. Seeing things that weren't there was okay. As long as she didn't cut. Vi wrote okay across and over all of the crazys on the page. It would have to be enough.

By the Saturday before the dorms were to close for winter break most of her pills were gone. She considered calling Dr. Gabriel for a prescription, something to keep the child away, at least during the day, but what would she say. That she was all better, except for these really lifelike hallucinations. Vi would have to manage through the break and try to figure something out later. On Monday she would have to leave Tubman's

Tower for the much maligned Home Away from Home camp, but she couldn't leave without attempting to see Dr. Locke. Tallahassee was more itself now that most of the students had returned to their origins, and Frenchtown Gardens fit its name. It looked like the pictures on postcards Vi had seen of Versailles. The ornate iron gates displayed an F and G on either side. It reminded her of The Centre in the way lovely things remind one of ugly things. From the outside The Centre could've easily been the head office for a small to middling insurance company. But this place had more in common with Perry's Club. The walk from the main street to the main house spanned at least a mile. The manicured hedges lining both sides of the road opened up into a circular driveway with a fountain reminiscent of Chicago's Buckingham Fountain. Vi wondered if that too had been a gift from our European cousins or was it just another copy. The double doors stood wide open, making Vi feel small as she stepped over the threshold. Vi approached a woman perched comfortably behind along counter.

"Welcome to Frenchtown Gardens. Your Respite from the World. May I help you?"

She wanted to tell her no and retrace her steps but knew she couldn't. "I'm here to visit Dr. Locke. I called earlier. My name is Viola Moon."

The receptionist looked down at a list that seemed to hold the answers to everything.

Certainly. Dr. Locke is," she looked at the list again, "in the Napoleon Room."

"Really?" She thought the girl must've been joking. The receptionist simply pointed to the second set of doors. Vi followed the direction of the clearly labeled halls until she reached the Napoleon Room. It was nothing like those places you see in movies; all white, with no sharp edges and residents in various ranges of sanity involved in nonsensical activities. Plush sitting chairs and loaded bookshelves filled the mahogany-paneled room. She found Dr. Locke at a small desk in the corner with leather-bound books covering the surface. He held one of the books open to the middle.

"Dr. Locke? It's me. Viola Moon."

He moved his glasses to the tip of his nose and peered over them, revealing all of his teeth. Was that happiness? She had never seen it before, and the grinning did make him look crazy. "Ms. Moon. What a wonderful surprise. Sit please. I've just gotten to my favorite part. My eyes aren't what they used to be. Would you mind reading a little for me?"

Vi was happy to have an assignment because her master plan to visit Dr. Locke had ended at the door. She had no idea what she was going to say to him or what she needed from him, so she began to read.

Nothing so aggravates an earnest person as a passive resistance. If the individual so resisted be of a not inhumane temper, and the resisting one perfectly harmless in his passivity, then, in the better moods of the former, he will endeavor charitably to construe to his imagination what proves impossible to be solved by his judgment. Even so, for the most part, I regarded Bartleby and his ways. Poor fellow! Thought I, he means no mischief; it is plain he intends no insolence; his aspect sufficiently evinces that his eccentricities are involuntary. He is useful to me. I can get along with him.

She stopped reading, but Locke nodded at her to continue.

If I turn him away, the chances are he will fall in with some less-indulgent employer, and then he will be rudely treated, and perhaps driven forth miserably to starve. Yes. Here I can cheaply purchase delicious self-approval. To befriend Bartleby; to humor him in his strange willfulness, will cost me little or nothing, while I lay up in my soul what will eventually prove a sweet morsel for my conscience. But this mood was not invariable with me. The passiveness of Bartleby sometimes irritated me.

I felt strangely goaded on to encounter him in new opposition - to elicit some angry spark from him answerable to my own. But, indeed, I might as well have essayed to strike fire with my knuckles against a bit of Windsor soap.

Vi closed the book, taking in the room in its entirety. "This collection is wonderful."

Locke closed his cloudy eyes. "Yes it is. Please keep reading."

As days passed on, I became considerably reconciled to Bartleby, his steadiness, his freedom from all dissipation, his incessant industry (except when he chose to throw himself into a standing revery behind his screen), his great stillness, his unalterableness of demeanor under all circumstances, made him a valuable acquisition. One prime thing was this - he was always there—first in the morning, continually through the day, and the last at night.

Vi stopped reading. This was a fiction. Bartleby did not exist. No one can live unaltered. Refusal to act could not keep one from being altered. That was a dream. If Vi could not distinguish the real versus the imagined, something would have to change. Change was always already. Dr. Locke was proof that change had to happen. Bartleby was a lie.

Vi stood up. "Dr. Locke, I have to get back."

"But you just got here. Please, I wanted to talk to you about the room."

"The room?"

"The books? Have they discovered them yet?"

It took a moment for Vi to realize Locke meant his books, not her own. She ran out of the Attic so quickly, she hadn't even thought to check on Locke's secret library, but Tunisia hadn't mentioned it. Surely if it had been discovered, Tunisia would've been foaming at the mouth to impart yet another sign of Dr. Locke's instability. She shook her head from side to side.

"I'm going to need you to move them. It's only a matter of time before that Cristabel and her cronies discover it. It's up to you now."

"Up to me. Dr. Locke I can't."

"Ms. Moon you must." He stood up. "You must."

"Dr. Locke. Please."

Locke's unfamiliar happiness disappeared, replaced with a look of both incredulity and panic. "What is wrong with you?" He stood up and moved closer to her chair, forcing her back into her seat. "I ask you to read one short story by one of America's most prolific writers, but you don't have time. I give you the opportunity to save the world, and you don't have time. What do you have to do that's so important?"

Vi was terrified. While in the Attic, at least Locke was bound by the artifice of his post. In this place, he was bound by nothing. Vi crouched so deeply into the seat, it tipped over, so she began to crawl toward the door

Locke continued to follow after her. "You lock a blind man in a library full of first editions. There is a special kind of hell for people like you. You did this didn't you Ms. Moon? You and that Ms. Johnson were in cahoots all along weren't you? You are responsible for me being here aren't you?"

When she finally made it into the hall, he stopped just shy of the door's inner threshold, as if some sort of force field blocked him from crossing over into the hall. "Don't worry Ms. Moon. This place will not hold me for long. I have tenure."

The men in scrubs appeared from nowhere, and the façade fell—the truth of Frenchtown Gardens revealed.

"I've got tenure. They can only hold me for so long. I will be back before you know it. Lovely visit Ms. Moon, please return. Please. I implore you. Return soon."

Vi got up and ran and didn't stop running until safely outside of the gates. She couldn't carry Heracles children. She was not Locke. They were not the same. His fate was not her fate. In the midst of contemplating her sanity, Vi spotted Perry across the street. He walked slowly, but purposefully. He seemed smaller, but she attributed his shrinkage to the distance between them. His hair stood out from his head like a puffy brown crown. When did he grow it out? He moved like a man of leisure, as if whoever he planned to meet would wait for him. She followed him from across the street, matching his pace. Even so, she still had to anticipate his moves to make sure he wouldn't see her following him. He made a left into Sheffield Park; a place the gainfully employed had abandoned a decade ago. It stood now as a haven for the indigent. He didn't stop. He made a direct line to the blood bank. Vi waited, but not alone. The child appeared alongside of her, waiting too. Not in her dreams, not in her reality, but somewhere in between. They didn't wait long. He came out with hands shoved deep into the pockets of his oversized gym shorts. Vi followed wondering what he traded his blood for. He passed the pawnshop and continued to the Seven Eleven. He went inside only to come out a few minutes later carrying a pint-sized brown bag. He turned the bag up to his lips, draining it quickly, before tossing the bag in the trash. Vi waited as Perry tried to make up his mind, trying to decide if the liquid courage had been enough. Then a girl approached him. She was chubbier than Vi, and hidden beneath a straight black wig. Vi never would've worn the crimson color staining her lips, but still the girl could've been Vi's close relation. Perry followed the girl behind the Seven Eleven and into the Motor Inn. So Perry still didn't know what he'd tried to take from her couldn't be taken, and it couldn't be bought either. What he just traded his blood for had to be given freely. He didn't know, so she waited so she could tell him. She wanted to tell him she knew he hadn't meant to pull her insides out between her legs, twist them into a fiery ball, and stuff it back into her. She wanted to tell him she forgave him, but she wouldn't get the chance because when Perry finally emerged from the motel room, it wasn't Perry. She'd been mistaken, again. The man who wasn't Perry turned and walked in the opposite direction, and this time, they didn't follow him.

Vi felt like the American Japanese must've felt in 1942 en route to Gila River. But this wasn't an interment camp. Her displacement wasn't forced. The dorms had to close for winter break, and she couldn't go home. Did that count as a choice? HAH. Home Away from Home. She shouldn't have lied to Cecilia. She shouldn't have told her she'd been invited home by her new best friend/roommate Danielle to spend Christmas break in Detroit. But return was impossible. The bus from A&M was only half full. They picked them up from the center of campus, right in front of Booker T.'s fountains. None of them talked on the bus. The only sounds emanated from the driver's shifting gears. Even the child remained quiet. Without the benefit of Ronnie's continual pill supply, the child had become Vi's constant companion, though lately the baby had become too weak to fully realize the screeching wails of her initial arrival. The absence of her jarring screams made her presence no less oppressing. Her deteriorating body remained a sign of Vi's perpetual failure. Vi was too afraid to consider what the child's death would mean for her own sanity. The books weren't working. They hadn't worked for Locke, and they hadn't worked for her.

Vi studied the changing landscape. Had they been driving 30 minutes or an hour? Vi couldn't judge. Why did they have to take them so far away? She watched the landscape change in the midst of that anxiousness that slows time when you are going to a place you've never been before when a huge billboard suddenly announced their arrival. **Home Away from Home: A Joint Project**. The bus turned into the unfinished driveway. The gravel crunched heavily against the bus' interior silence.

The as yet speechless driver spoke. "Home away from home." He laughed.

Vi grabbed her belongings and descended into the dust kicked up by the influx. Cabin-like buildings peppered a dusty ravine; each plopped down in no apparent relation to another, as if designed by a band of myopics. Evergreens had been cut back to create a circular perimeter, serving as an orderly border to the scattered confusion.

"Check in at the trailer. You'll get your cabin assignments. Happy Holidays." The closing bus door muffled the driver's laughter.

A woman with a clipboard stood on the small raised deck outside of the welcome trailer. Since there was only room for one on the deck, she was forced to look down on all who approached her. "Name and School?"

"Viola Moon. A&M University."

"Moon, moon. You're in Hut 25."

"Hut?"

"Yes, Hut 25. It's right next to Hut 24. The latrines and showers are to the right." She nodded her head toward her left. "And the mess hall is in The Mansion through the center of camp. Dinner is at 4pm sharp. Be late and be hungry." She looked up from her clipboard. Vi assumed the open space was for questions. They tumbled over each other inside of her head. Could she ever really go home? What would happen if the child died? Would she ever be able to forgive Perry?

"Next. Name and School?" The woman on deck looked down at the boy behind her.

Vi's interior dialogue and exterior silence had obviously gobbled all of her allotted time, so she moved out of line and in the direction of the woman's nod. It took her 30 minutes to find Hut 25. At HAH everything was relative, especially phrases like "next to" and "hut." The hut was actually a square cinder block structure. It felt and smelled like a basement above ground. It made her room in Tubman's Tower feel like one of those overdone soft places spread between the covers of glossy magazines. The waterbugs were more at home on her cot than she could ever be, but she managed to clear them to make room for her suitcase. She emptied her backpack onto the worn desk. The empty envelope with Perry's name sat on top. The child's silent hunger was absorbed by the untreated cinderblock, and Vi heard it without hearing it like her own heartbeat. Place didn't matter. This was Vi's legacy. Vi sat down at the desk. She had to write the letter she'd been struggling to write for weeks.

Dear Perry,

I am not sure why you continue to hurt me. I love   . I want to love you. I want to be what you need me to be. You refuse to see me. I see you. I have my father's eyes. Diana thinks I am fatherless. But I am not. I am a Moon. My father is a Moon, and his father is a Moon. I have proof. I am not a nigger. I am not a nigger. You put something in me and I need you to take it back. I cannot continue to drag your sin behind me. You need to take it. I love   . I want to love you. Let me. See me. Like I see you. I have my father's eyes. She has my father's eyes. Diana was wrong. Dr. Gabrielle was wrong. I am not a nigger.

She signed it Viola Ikewke Moon, and sealed it in an envelope. Something deep inside of her began to grumble, drowning out the child's hunger. She looked at the clock on the wall. It was ten minutes until four.

Vi entered The Mansion unprepared for the aged opulence. Her sneakers landed soundlessly on the inlaid mahogany floor. The ballroom needed no introduction. The double doors opened to sky-high ceilings lit by crystal chandeliers. The temporariness of the banquet tables only highlighted the brilliance of the room's hardscapes. She grabbed a tray and watched as a student worker with long blonde dreads piled it high with what some would consider traditional holiday fare. Vi hadn't realized the depth of her hunger until then. As the girl baptized the plate with a ladle of gravy, Vi's stomach grumbled again.

"And it's as good as it looks." The girl with the blonde dreads winked.

Vi took her food and moved into the center of the temporary tables. She walked toward a cluster of A&M's students, and then she remembered. They didn't belong to her; not there and not here, so she walked over to a table in front of one of the windows. The ten-foot French windowpanes cut the landscape into perfect parcels. A pair of floor to ceiling purple velvet brocade drapes that Scarlet could have made a gaggle of gowns out of lined both sides of each window. The parceled views in between stood in stark contrast to the fabric's velvety lushness. The land, unlike A&M, lay flat, leaving the view to the huts unencumbered. Vi stared, trying to decode the pattern of their random placement, she hardly noticed the girl now sitting across from her. She might've seen her at check-in.

"Crazy right? They say the cabins are placed in the exact corresponding coordinates of the big and little dipper. Who knows? You'd have to be on much higher ground to verify that report. Even then those dusty cellblocks would probably just blend into the dust around them."

"You could put a light at the top of each one."

"Yeah, I guess that would make 'em more visible at least at night."

"You work here?"

"Me? No. You a freshman?" Her eyebrows went up into an arch. "At A&M? Connie. I'm a junior at State. This is my third time at HAH."

"Vi." She had no other words to fill in the empty space, so she took another bite of her mashed potatoes.

"This was Tallahassee's attempt at socialism." Connie nodded toward the ceiling.

Vi glanced up at the crystal chandeliers that hung from each corner of the room. The ceiling's fading frescoes were barely visible under the multiple points of light reflecting back onto them.

"See." Connie pointed up. "You see them all working the land. Blueblood and Commoner alike."

Vi followed her finger. It rested on a woman with a hoe in her left hand. The hoe was also held in the right hand of another woman. The second woman was identical to the first except her face was painted white. "Socialism?"

"Every socialist camp needs a ballroom." Connie laughed at her own joke. The potatoes stuck to all sides of her mouth.

"Why didn't you go home?"

"No home to go to. My old man moves a lot."

Vi wanted to ask about her old lady. She had to have a mother. Vi couldn't imagine her life without a Cecilia Before or Cecilia After. But she understood the danger of questions, so she shoveled a gravy-encrusted fork full of turkey into her mouth.

The girl scrunched up her nose. "How can you eat that?"

"You don't eat meat?"

"Nope. Nothing with a mother."

"What about with a father?"

The girl cocked her head to one side, looking at Vi as if she'd grown another head. "Yeah. Same thing." Connie's eyes began hopping around the room, and landed on the blonde girl with dreadlocks. "Anyway, I'll see you around." She picked up her tray of motherless food and moved to the girl's table.

Vi looked down at her plate. The gravy had grown into a sea, encompassing everything on her plate, and she suddenly lost her appetite.

Time crept at HAH. Ironically, the child's hunger became Vi's only reprieve from the monotony of solitude and sameness. The child's erratic reappearances stood in abject opposition to HAH's habitual schedule. Wake-up bell at 8 am, baby at 8:01, breakfast at 8:30, baby at 9:23, write letter to Perry at 10 am, baby at 11:42 am, lunch at noon, tear up letter at 1:10 pm. For three weeks she wrote and then destroyed her letters, mostly under the watchful eyes of the child. Each day as alike and unlike the next, until finally, electric yellow pieces of paper posted everywhere announcing the camps final Going Away Party. The winter break was at its end, and everyone would be returned to their respective campuses soon. In anticipation of the impending celebration, the camp seemed to erupt; Mardi Gras in December. Though she had found neither the motivation or the means to enter any of the clumps at HAH, she did like to observe them from a distance on nightly walks. One of her favorite spots to stop and observe was the old playground. It had been built after the grounds had become a haven for naturalists. As she settled in on the swings, raucous voices announced themselves from the path between The Mansion and the huts, so Vi moved to a more obscure point of observation behind the monkey bars. The laughter settled far enough away that Vi could observe without participation. She imagined this is what Dian Fossey must've felt, until, alas, human nature's drive to be a part pushed her toward the center and contaminated every thing thereafter.

Hard laughter sliced the cool night air into thick frigid strips. "I'm not a Dyke." The girl tossed her long blond loc over her shoulder. Her lips glistened under the small circle of light shining from the sole streetlight over the playground.

Why only one light in a playground? Did naturalists like to play in the dark?

"What?" The second voice rose from the darkness. Because Vi had subsisted in virtual silence for the last three weeks, she easily placed the voice. The girl who only ate parentless food. Due to the clarity of her voice, Connie must've been sitting on one of the dilapidated swings Vi had just vacated.

"Are you deaf? I'm not a dyke."

A blonde boy, whose arm must have always been around the blonde girl's waist, came into full view, pulling her in the opposite direction. "You couldn't have found a hot girl to mess around with?"

The shiny-lipped girl moved out of the small circle of artificial light in a cloud of giggles, and Connie took the girl's place in the center of light, watching them leave. Vi shifted and sound echoed. Connie's eyes moved across the playground like a roach scurrying for fleeting food and found Vi. The mist had risen. She'd been spotted by one of the gorillas. Unlike Fossey, Vi attempted to minimize the contamination by walking away, but this gorilla had no intention of making escape easy.

"Hey. Wait." Connie ran walked over to Vi. "A&M right?"

"Vi."

"Hey Vi. What you up to?" A neediness dangled from the question that Vi attempted to ignore.

"Walking."

"Want some company?"

Vi wanted to say no, but it would be a lie. The solitude of the last three weeks pushed her shoulders into a shrug, and Connie fell into line next to her. They followed the circle of pines around the camp. Neither spoke.

After 45 minutes, her knees ached, so Vi stopped in front of her hut. "I'm tired."

"Me too." But the gorilla didn't take the hint and leave. Instead it stood, staring at the entrance to Hut 25.

Vi made no move forward. She fought the urge to shoo the creature away like Cecilia would shoo the feral cats that would sometimes drift into the backyard.

"You mind if I stay. I hate being alone. I'll sleep on the floor. I don't care."

Only the basest of human decency prevented her from being rude to the only person who'd spoken to her in three weeks. "Okay."

While Connie made a pallet from almost nothing on the hard floor, Vi climbed into her cot, unsealed her last revision of her letter to Perry and began the revisions. It was her contribution to HAH's schedule of sameness. Each night she would unseal it, and reread what she wrote earlier, marking through what had made sense, but was now undecipherable. The letter looked like one of Locke's lists. More red than black and white. Sometimes the baby watched, sometimes she didn't. This time Vi read alone, except, of course, for Connie who watched from the floor as Vi wrote over her former revisions. She was in the midst of ripping the letter up when pain radiating from her navel interrupted her.

"Are you okay?" Connie stood up, blocking the only light in the room night with her wide frame.

Vi nodded. Words could not be trusted, and the pain sitting at the base of her spine made the air difficult to handle.

"You want me to rub your back."

Vi wanted to say no, but the knife twisting in her spine made her nod yes.

"Lay on your side." Connie's hands were strong and sure as they sought out the pain. "Is it here?"

Vi held her breath in response.

"Close your eyes and breathe."

Vi followed Connie's instructions and exhaled. The knife retreated, and she relaxed into Connie's strong hands. The exhaustion of all that had come before finally caught up to her and she drifted into sleep.

Vi woke up in an unfamiliar room. Not the unfamiliarity of Tubman Tower 203D, but a new place she didn't belong to. It felt wrong. But when she looked around, her things were everywhere. The doll Cecilia had given her that had once been her grandmother's. The picture of her parents. Through the window, the swingset she'd gotten on her 6th birthday. The things in this place belonged to her, but Vi didn't belong to this place. She could hear Cecilia singing in the shower. The running water drowned out the words, but the voice was unmistakable. So she ran to the bathroom and pulled back the shower curtain. Cecilia turned toward her, but her mouth was missing. Scars, raised and dark, like the Appalachian mountains on the relief map Cecilia had helped her make in 3rd grade, formed a an x across her chest. Vi covered her eyes and backed out of the bathroom. Her faceless father picked her up and carried her out of the house. A heavy screen of smoke disguised the way out. Cecilia.

"Daddy wait Cecilia will burn."

"Don't worry baby. She's going to a better place."

"But Daddy."

"It's you and me now Tommy."

"Daddy, who's Tommy?" But he kept walking like he didn't hear her. "Daddy. Answer me. Please. Daddy. Answer me."

"Vi. Shit wake up. You okay. You're going to wake up the whole damn camp." Connie pushed her stringy hair back from her face with thick fingers, moving onto the edge of Vi's cot.

"I had a dream. My father. He set my house on fire. It was awful. He kept calling me Tommy."

Connie blew a long slow breath of air, pulling her wet t-shirt away from her body. "Shit. Sorry."

"For what?"

"I talk in my sleep. I must've been talking in my sleep again."

"What?"

"Vi, I'm Tommy."

"What?"

"Thomasina. After my father. Constance's my middle name. I was in a fire when I was little. It was some real scary shit. Sometimes I relive it in my sleep. It hasn't happened for a while. With all the excitement earlier. You know. Sorry." Connie shrugged.

"Your father set the fire?"

"What? No of course not. If it wasn't for him saving me, we all would've burned."

Were Vi's dreams that susceptible to revision? She didn't even know this strange girl, and yet she had shared a dream with her, a dream as real as the emaciated child sitting in the corner of Hut 25. Vi thought she'd left it behind. Dr. Gabrielle told her she had to leave it behind.

— *When my mother first met her mother, she ran.*

— *Who ran? Cecilia or her mother?*

— *Cecilia.   She was sitting on the stoop in front of her aunt's greystone when she smelled strawberries. A lady pushed the rusty iron gate and it made this sound that sounded like run to Cecilia. When the lady's high heels moved across the concrete walk leading to the stoop, it sounded like run. When the lady said, "Stand up child, and give your momma a kiss," it all sounded like run to her. So that's what she did. Cecilia jumped off the stoop and ran straight through that gate. She didn't know where she was going, but she ran as hard and fast as she could. By the time she passed the candy store, the pink ribbons her aunt had put in her hair that morning were streaming behind her. Her throat rattled with dry heaves, and the muscles in her legs started to restrict, but she kept running. Her heart felt like it was going to explode from her chest, but she kept running.*

— *When did she finally stop?*

—

— *Vi, when did she stop running?*

— *She stopped when it hurt more to keep going than it did to stand still.*

—

—

— *Did Cecilia tell you that story?*

— *No.*

— *Who told you?*

—

— *Vi?*

— *I think I dreamt it.*

— *That's not possible. Did Cecilia tell you that story?*

—

— *Did Cecilia tell you that story?*

— *I don't know. I can't remember. What does it matter? What's the difference anyway if she did or didn't?*

—   *Vi   the difference is everything.*

"Shit it's hot as hell in here and my shirt is soaked." Connie pulled her t-shirt over her head, leaving her white breasts exposed. Connie's eyes followed Vi's as she stood up and wiped her armpits with her wet t-shirt. "You got a t-shirt I can borrow?"

Vi did not move from her place on the cot. She couldn't stop staring at the girl's breasts. The pink tips reminded her of the plastic baby bottle nipples you can buy at the local drugstore, unmarked and unnatural.

"What?"

"I've never seen a white girl's."

"I can't stand bras. Too uncomfortable. I don't see why I should be uncomfortable just to make someone else more comfortable. Are they that different?"

Vi shrugged.

Connie nodded as if making note for later trivia reference. "You want to touch them. I don't care. Go ahead."

As Vi reached out with her left hand, she knew she was about to cross a line that even Dian Fossey would've left etched in place. She cupped them with both hands, as if trying to hold water. So captivated with the round heaviness of each breast, she was shocked when Connie moved in to kiss her.

Vi dropped Connie's breasts and jumped back. She had gotten too close to the natives. She had done more than just contaminate her research. "What are you doing?"

"What do you mean? I thought."

"You thought wrong." Something boiled up inside of Vi as she found herself repeating the words of the shiny-lipped girl. "I'm not a dyke." She pushed through the door, letting the screen slam behind her. The night air felt cool as it moved down Vi's back. Why was she so angry? Connie had done nothing wrong really. She just needed. Was that it? The burden of one more person's fucked up repressed history. Didn't she have enough to carry? Wasn't the child enough? Vi found the matches in her jacket pocket. She couldn't remember where or how she'd acquired them. She looked at the cover. The Brief Encounter. Had she carried this for that long? It had only been a few months, but it seemed like decades, no centuries. She walked to the camp's entrance, nothing but miles of dusty road back to A&M. What was she going to do, walk back to campus? What difference would that make? The child had followed her. The child couldn't be vanquished by place, and her dreams didn't just belong to her and Cecilia. Their connection was not special or magical. The aged sign announcing this place appeared in front of her like a dare. Home Away From Home: A Joint Project. The inhaled smoke from Connie's dream clouded her reason. The Brief Encounter matches lit easily, and the splintered oak burned just as easily. The sign disappeared and she watched. The second Home moved into completely blackness by the time she had tired of watching the wood melt into black soot, and by the time she returned to Hut 25, it was gorilla free.

Vi never imagined she would be glad to see Tubman's Towers. Everything was just as she'd left it. Vi walked around the room touching the things she left behind. Her Moons had begun to creep onto Danielle's side right before Thanksgiving. Now they climbed to the top of both bookshelves, across Danielle's abandoned cot, filling both closets. "You need him to feed you too." Vi didn't remember when the words had left her head and caught air, but somewhere between HAH and Tubman's Tower she began to talk to the child. She spoke to her because it kept her quiet. Vi discovered either in her sleep or her awakening the child seemed soothed, if not satiated, by her voice. As she settled back into her bed, her abdomen contracted, and she doubled over in pain. The cramps had been coming in waves for over a week, but the blood never followed. She looked at the box of unused tampons on her dresser. When was the last time? The whimpering began again and Vi's focus shifted. She was fooling herself if she thought her lone voice would ever be enough to soothe   ? What should she call her? Would calling her keep her here? Had Cecilia called her something before she'd buried her? Vi could not remember the last time she'd heard Cecilia's voice. Vi needed to demand the truth. She had to tell Cecilia neither this child nor her questions were going to go away.

— Cecilia?

— Vi. Is that you? Are you okay? Why didn't you call me over the break? I've been so

— Worried?

— No. Not worried. I just wanted to hear your voice. This is our first time being

— Not together.

— Yes. Apart. Did you have a good time in Detroit?

— Of course. Danielle's family is perfect. Everything was perfect.

—

— Cecilia? Are you still there?

— Yes.

—

— How are you sleeping?

—   Fine.

— Good.   Will you be coming home for Spring Break?

—

— Vi? Are you coming home?

— If I can. Cecilia. I need to go now. I'm late for work.

— How is Dr.   ?

— Locke.

— Yes. Dr. Locke.

—   Fine.

—

— Cecilia don't worry. Everything is perfect. I have to go. I will call you again soon.

Vi hung up the phone and ran back to 203D. Her demands dissipated the moment she heard Cecilia After's voice. Questions only pushed them further away from each other. Cecilia wasn't ready to hear Vi's truth. She needed to believe everything was better for Vi at A&M. Everything in due time. Dr. Gabrielle had taught her that.

    — *Vi, it's time.*

    —

    — *It's time to talk about it.*

    —

    — *What do you want to know?*
    — *How about we start with the cicadas?*
    — *Cicadas?*

    —

    —

    —

    — *They were everywhere. You know they come out every seventeen years. I went outside for something. I can't remember, but I do remember one on my back. It wouldn't fly away. I hate bugs, and these things are the fattest ugliest loudest bugs I've ever seen. I finally had to take off my shirt to get that ugly thing off me and once I got that thing off of me I was in kill mode. I mean I overkilled it. I smashed it into a cicada pancake. Jelly and all. Disgusting. But afterwards I felt so powerful   but I was naked, at least from the waist up, and there they were, in front of me, mocking me. I wanted to smash them like I had done that croaking thing. I wanted to show them they wouldn't do to me what they did to Cecilia.*

    —

    — *So I filled up the bathtub and cut.*
    — *And you did it because of the cicadas?*
    — *I did it because I didn't want to die, and I knew they were going to kill me. That they were going to kill me exactly like they killed Cecilia.*
    — *But Cecilia's not dead.*
    — *I know that.*
    — *But you said they killed Cecilia.*

    —

    —

    — *Slip of the tongue. I meant almost killed her.*

— *Did you?*

— *Are you suggesting I think my mother is dead?*

—

—   *Maybe part of her*

— *Maybe part of her what? Why did you stop?*

— *She changed after. But how does that happen to you and nothing change.*

— *So how did her change, change your relationship?*

—

—

— *Cecilia and me were like   it's hard to explain. We were like each other. Like sometimes we wouldn't talk to each other for days, but not cause we were angry or mad. Because we didn't need. Words. We didn't need words.*

— *And after the cancer?*

— *What?*

—

— *It was just different. And I'd rather cut them off, before I let cancer make it even worse.*

Noises from the hall interrupted her memory. They were happy noises. Noises girls who missed each other made when reunited. She shut the door. She shut the door and comforted the child.

CHAPTER SEVENTEEN

The footsteps vibrating from the room next door sounded different. Each step expressed an urgency Cecilia couldn't remember hearing before. Cecilia wanted to stop her; to tell her she wasn't ready to leave; to go a thousand miles away to a place she'd never been; it was too soon after. But watching her pull a trunk full of everything she valued, Cecilia wanted to cry. Vi was seventeen. It seemed like a decade since her last birthday when the husks of new cicadas peppered the driveway. Dr. Gabrielle assured her Vi wouldn't repeat the unthinkable. Cecilia wanted to be as certain as Dr. Gabrielle, but she wasn't. Vi assured her she was fine. But the words lay meaningless in the space between them. Cecilia wanted to grab Vi and her things and drag them both back into her room.

The first night back from the Centre, Cecilia asked Vi if she wanted to sleep with her, and Vi had looked at her with such pity. "I'm fine. Cecilia. I'm used to being alone." Cecilia fought the urge to grab and press her head against the soft place, but the soft place had been cut away. So instead of stopping her, Cecilia helped Vi drag the trunk to the front door.

CHAPTER EIGHTEEN

They were waiting for her. The Attic was lit up like Christmas. Lights she never noticed before beamed into every corner of the sub-basement, leaving no shadows. Who knew the Attic held the potential for such an overwhelming brightness. Mrs. Lattimore and Tunisia sat to the right of Dr. Cristabel in a semicircle like Vi and the others had been encouraged to do at the Centre. An empty seat faced the semicircle. Vi assumed they were saving it for her.

"Viola. Please. Take a seat." Dr. Cristabel's pleasant expression didn't reach aher eyes as she nodded toward Mrs. Lattimore.

Mrs. Lattimore opened a manila folder sitting on her full lap.

Vi didn't know whether to sit or run, but the exhaustion enveloping her made the decision for her, and she collapsed into the chair.

All three women stared at Vi's stomach.

A slow wicked smirk crept across Tunisia's face. "I told you this Bama got knocked up. What an idiot."

Dr. Cristabel shot Tunisia a look, which erased the evil grin. "Viola. Mrs. Lattimore has brought some disturbing things to my attention regarding your work here at the Library. Present condition aside," she nodded toward Vi's stomach, "we need to focus on other matters."

Present condition? Could Dr. Cristabel see the child? Was this private nightmare finally public? Did this mean they would send her back to the Centre? "You can see the baby?"

"Of course Viola. You must be what? Six, seven months along."

What was she talking about? This baby was years beyond gestation. Both fully-formed and deteriorating. They were still as blind as Locke. There would be no rescue. There would be no condemnation. Vi shrunk back into herself. They couldn't see.

"Viola. Let me get to the point of this meeting." Mrs. Lattimore handed Dr. Cristabel the file. "There are several books missing."

Vi shrugged. "Shrinkage has been a problem since before I started working here."

Dr. Cristabel's studied Vi's calm face. "The numbers are triple the libraries ordinary shrinkage estimates. There are even books missing from the Attic. How do you explain those?"

Tunisia stared at Vi, barely camouflaging her joy in the inquisition.

Vi realized Tunisia's antipathy had never been personal. She was simply a gazer; the bloodthirsty crowd in the Greek arena; the picnickers at Southern lynchings, the subject defining the object, but Vi didn't want to be object to Tunisia's subject, and she wouldn't give up her Moons. She didn't have a choice. She had to give them something, and the only thing she had to give them was Locke. "I'm sorry Dr. Cristabel. I should have said something earlier. But with Dr. Locke's   — illness. Tunisia took them."

Tunisia's antipathy became self-righteous shock. "What would I want with all those books?"

Vi directed all of her answers to Dr. Cristabel. "She told me her plan to set Dr. Locke up. She wanted to get him gone permanently, and there was some rule about criminal charges being the only way to revoke tenured faculty."

Dr. Cristabel hesitated, looking at Mrs. Lattimore. Mrs. Lattimore shrugged. They both turned toward Tunisia.

Tunisia began to boil beneath their gaze. "That's not what I said. I said it was a damn shame Dr. Locke could do damn near anything he wanted and still have a job. What about you?" Tunisia turned toward Dr. Cristabel and Mrs. Lattimore. "She had sex up in the stacks. I saw her. That's probably when she got knocked up."

Vi continued to direct her comments directly to Dr. Cristabel. "That's true. It's what she was holding over me. When I told her to stop, she told me she would report me. I was — embarrassed." Vi looked down toward the floor. "I should have said something. She has the books hidden in an old storage room down here somewhere. I'm not sure where."

Dr. Cristabel's frozen forehead wrinkled. "Well. It looks as if we are going to have to take some time to further investigate this. For now, Viola and Tunisia, you both need to take some time off until we figure this out."

Vi never lifted her eyes from the floor. Even as she ascended the stairs leading from the Attic, she continued to watch her step. She knew it was only a matter of time before they discovered her lie and dealt with her accordingly. Once they found Locke's lair they would know Tunisia didn't possess the ability to so carefully catalogue those doomed books. Her dorm room would be next. 203D. She hadn't been to most of her classes since winter break, so dismissal from school was already a foregone conclusion, but what would happen to them if she lost her books? The child traveled alongside, bones barely covered by wasting skin. They would make her go back. They said they could see the child too, but could they? The sun, as bright as that first day in autumn, followed them to Booker T.'s Four Fountains. Pistons of water shot out of hidden sources, splashing her face. It smelled second hand, as if recycled from some underground pool. She turned her face away from the rhythmic spurts, suddenly noticing the cold brisk air opposing the sun's persistence. Vi teetered on the edge of the fountain staring up at Booker T.'s lips frozen in reprimand. She felt as if she should apologize. Was she a credit to the race? Vi stared down at her worn running shoes. No bootstraps. What was she supposed to grab a hold of? The flagstone felt colder as the bottom of her jeans collected the reused water Booker T. discarded. Three small shrill noises cut through the brisk air. The three chirps were answered by three more. They seemed to descend from heaven. Brown angels cloaked in white and silver floated about, taping and posting silver and white feathers on everything within reach.

"Isn't that your roommate?" One of them said to another.

One of the angels moved closer, and Danielle's pretty face came into focus. Danielle. Still never alone. She must have gone over. "Vi?" Danielle's eyes rested on Vi's protruding abdomen. "You shouldn't be out here without a jacket or something. It's not Chicago, but it's not Miami either."

Vi nodded in response, afraid that Danielle would vanish if she said anything.

"Come on. I'll walk you back."

Vi let Danielle pull her to her feet, and walk her back to Tubman's

Towers with the child trailing closely behind them.

When she opened the door to 203D, Danielle surveyed the Moons in silence.

Vi felt the need to explain. "I had to take them. They're all Moons."

Danielle examined all of the once empty spaces only to find them all brimming over with even more Moons.

Vi shrugged. "It's only a matter of time before they come to take them back."

Danielle pressed her lips together and avoided Vi's eyes. "Come on, let's get you out of those wet clothes." Danielle grabbed a towel off the back of the door and led her to the bathroom across the hall from 203D. She must've thought that Booker T.'s baptism was piss. Vi didn't try to explain. She just let Danielle help her out of the wet jeans that would no longer button around her middle, and into the shower. It felt good to be cared for. The towel dropped to the floor, and Danielle's eyes found the question mark cradling Vi's heart.

How could Vi explain why she'd carved a question into her chest? It would just run her back out of her room, and she didn't want to be alone with the child. "I don't like to talk about it."

Danielle's veil dropped as she pressed her lips together again. "I understand." She pulled up her silver and white-flecked jersey, revealing a pyramid of small straight lines right underneath her navel. Danielle was a Carver. She should've known it from the beginning. Vi reached out without thinking and touched them. The cuts were rigid and healed over, but at Vi's touch, the veil fell back over Danielle's face, and she dropped her shirt. She sparkled the same way as the first day they'd met. Had it been as synthetic back then? Danielle walked her back into 203D, and helped her into a clean and dry pair of sweats. "Are you feeling better? Do you want me to stay?"

Vi wrapped herself in her grandmother's quilt. "I have class in an hour. I'll be fine."

Danielle delivered an understanding nod and bounced out of the room, leaving more than her secret behind. It was one of the feathers her sorority had been posting all over campus. A flyer announcing the 8pm sale of the man who had tried to render her invisible.

Sound traveled faster than light. She heard the clanking of chains centuries before she caught the glint of steel against black flesh. She and the baby pushed their way through the throng of feverish bidders. The boy on the stage glowered, flexing his arms in response to the auctioneer's encouragement. Up close the truth of the chains became clearer. She couldn't have heard metal grating against metal because the chains were plastic, but the shirtless exposed body was real. She could smell the sweat glistening across his skin. He fell to the floor and began to do push-ups, first with both hands, and then with only the right one. The bidders hooted and pushed their palms together. The auctioneer's mouth spread in a glossy smirk. The bidding started high and ended high. He was a fine specimen; bred for pleasure the auctioneer purported. Vi rubbed her moist palms down the sides of her sweats. White paddles engraved with thick black numbers waved wildly across the dank dance floor. A storm of giggles erupted from a group of girls as one of them was announced the winner. The specimen leaped from the stage, throwing himself into the arms of his new master. Perry was next. He stepped up on the auction block the way his great great-grandfather would've if he'd ever been a slave, reticent but proud. His eyes followed the path of his own feet as if trying to record every action and reaction. The auctioneer began to espouse his bloodlines. A legacy. His rough hands were joined together by toy chains, yet she could feel the heaviness, of both the chains and his hands. He was a legacy. It was what had convinced her of her love for him. He took something from her. The bidding started low; obviously this crowd didn't care about bloodlines. They cared about what you could lift. And Perry could barely hold up the weight of the toy chains. Why was she here? Why couldn't she walk away from him? The keloid burned around her breast. She rubbed her moist palms down the sides of her sweats again while the child's hunger emitted a steady hum under the noise of the crowd. She had to be here. They were coming for her Moons soon. They were not enough anyway. She had been fooling herself. She couldn't allow him to render her invisible. He had to see her. As if reading her thoughts, he stop recording the path of his feet and lifted his head. She saw him see her, and her visibility shrunk him. She stood too far away to catch him this time. She watched from the middle of the dance-floor as he fell to the ground uninterrupted by her need to save him.

His first word to her after stuffing something between her legs and months of refusing to see her was Stop. But he didn't and she wouldn't. She was the highest bidder. Who wanted a weak slave? Turns out he had not fallen purely from the strength of her visibility. His tumble had been aided by several shots of G-Nu punch. So glad to be rid of his weakness and her protruding belly, his fraternity brothers had even helped her load him into the backseat of Blue Thunder. They'd been glad to be able to return to the party and their traditions unencumbered by antagonists. Stop he said over and over before he began screaming it. But his screams only fueled her resolved. She knew she couldn't stop, so she pushed the car toward the beginning or the beginning of the end for Perry and her. She headed back to Albany while Perry passed out in a small pool of his own vomit.

The Cannons were in the process of waking up when she pulled up across the street from the Cannon house right before dawn. Perry's breathing sounded even from the back seat, so Vi left him in the car. As Vi approached the veranda, Cleo appeared as if summoned with a cup in her hand. Vi watched as the older woman contemplated the approaching sunset from the chaise. Vi also watched as the gardener moved from the other side of the veranda and sat at Cleo's feet. He removed her slippers before kissing each foot, and then her thighs and then in the place her thighs met. She watched as Cleo continued to contemplate the sunset, and sip from the steamless cup in her hand. Though Cleo's eyes hadn't closed, the gardener was invisible to her. Just like Perry had tried to make Vi invisible. Vi moved to the edge of the veranda, abandoning the cover of the wall of blue spruce, waiting for the gardener to return to whatever else he did in the light of day. When he completed his task and disappeared around the back of the property, Vi cleared her throat.

Cleo stopped contemplating the now risen sun. Her teacup tottered as she tried to place it on the side table. "I didn't hear anyone drive up. You startled me." Her eyes moved over Vi's shoulder. "Has my Perry decided to surprise me?"

"No."

"Is Perry alright?" There was no real alarm in her voice.

"He's fine. Drunk. Passed out in the car." Vi nodded toward the road.

Cleo rested back in her seat. A sardonic grimace crossed her face. "His mother's child I guess." She lifted the cup to her lips.

"I came here because I need."

"A father for your child."

"How did you know?" Could she see the child next to her, or was she like the rest, referring to a child that didn't yet exist? "Perry doesn't want me anymore Cleo. I can't get him to see me like he did before. I want to go back to how it was before   ."

"Before. Don't we all. We want to go back when we were younger, prettier,   freer. It's the nature of what comes before child. An unrealizable goal, but it's all we have."

Was she right? Was before all they had? How was that possible? "What about now?"

"What?" Cleo turned her head as if she was listening to something else.

Vi kneeled in front of her chair. "Now. I want now to be like before. Is that possible?"

She looked at Vi with a confused expression on her face. "What are you talking about? Now is now."

Vi had hoped this woman had something to offer her; an answer of how to move forward. Vi stood to leave when something moved on the other side of the French door.

"Only farmers and whores are up at this hour, and I don't hear any tractors." Diana clumped onto the veranda with one platform on and one in her hand. Her perfectly applied makeup had expired, and dark shadows hung under her eyes. "Oh it's Perry's Revenge." Diana sat down next to her mother and assessed Vi from head to toe. Her bitter laughter rang out over the waking house. "He's gone and done it again." She poured a cup of tea. "Please tell me you aren't just going to blindly accept this bastard as your own."

Vi began to back off of the veranda, but the car seemed miles away.

Diana continued her tirade. "Perry can just drag any little thing in here and knock her up, and you welcome it and her with open arms."

Vi was confused. They were talking about the child like it was both here and not. Both Perry's and not. This child was here, and it belonged only to her. "What are you talking about?"

"Who do you think you are dealing with you little gold-digging pickaninny. You'll get what that other one got. $300 and a ride home from the clinic. I know all about you Viola Moon. I know all about you and your people."

Just as Diana disappeared into the house, Perry stumbled onto the veranda, smelling of sweat and vomit. "Mother, don't worry. I'm not making you a grandmother any time soon. That's not my child."

"Of course it's not. The child is mine. She belongs only to me." Vi must not have said it out loud, because Cleo kept talking to Perry as if she had not said anything.

"Perry how can you be so sure?"

Perry leaned against the aged railing to steady himself. His head bounced forward like someone sleeping sitting up. "Because Mother, I can't have children."

Cleo laughed. "Of course you can. That little thing from the other side proved that."

Perry lifted his head and smiled at his mother. It was probably the first real smile she'd ever seen on his face. "She did, and I after that scare, I had a vasectomy."

Cleo almost knocked over her chair standing up. "What? How could you?"

"I decided that seven Perry Cannon's were more than enough." He turned toward Vi. "So you see Ms. Moon, this child could not be a Cannon. I'm afraid you've kidnapped me for nothing."

Diana reappeared. "There he is. The golden child. Just thought you might want to know that your little girlfriend is a liar. Her father isn't dead. He's alive and kicking in the middle of some Hicksville town in Alabama. Probably somewhere waiting for her to get some sort of big payoff." Diana began to laugh loud enough to wake every Cannon in Hangman's Hall. "Just a small investment of time with some very public records. I wonder what I could find out if I actually gave a damn." She threw the paper at Vi. "Go away, little peopleless girl." Diana turned as Cleo sank back into her chair. "Mother, what's wrong?"

Cleo shook her head, placing her hand over her heart. "How could he?"

But Vi was already back in the car. Diana had given her more than she could have wished for. These people had nothing. Right in front of her on the paper his full name, Ellington Moon. Alive and living in Elysia, Alabama. She had to go. The child's eyes now protruded from her skull from hunger, but the message was clear. Go.

The pain that began at the base of her spine months before had become more consistent and sharp. Vi pointed the car and headed toward Alabama. Time was running out, and Ellington Moon was alive.

CHAPTER NINETEEN

The soft voice hesitated on the other end of the phone. The caller I.D. displayed a Florida area code, but it wasn't Vi. It was her roommate. The roommate told Cecilia what she already knew. Her second chance child wasn't okay. Cecilia hung up the phone, picked it up again and dialed the airline. She waited without patience as the reservations line broadcasted a soulless version of We Are Family. No matter the cost. She had to go.

"Are you okay?"

"Of course not." Her brown eyes opened to green ones surrounded by wrinkles carved from years of laughter.

He chuckled, affirming her theory. "I'm sorry for waking you, but you were   talking in your sleep and you seemed…"

She waited.

"You seemed   to be having quite a time of it."

Cecilia blinked slowly not wanting to recall the time that rested uneasily on the other side of wakefulness. She recognized his need to know she was comfortably settled on this side. "All these years. Who knew I was a talker?" Her giggle in return seemed to assure him.

Ellington told her she talked in her sleep, but she never wanted to believe him. Thought it was an excuse. From the moment he chose her, she knew it wouldn't be forever. He was too beautiful. Too kind. Fell in love too quick. She simply didn't trust it. So when he finally said he had to leave, she was crushed and relieved. His departure meant she could finally relax into her broken heart in a way she'd never been able to relax into his love.

The altered voice emanating from the insufficient speaker interrupted. The weather was a perfect 78 degrees in Tallahassee. Clear skies. Had she enjoyed her flight? Would she enjoy her stay?

Smiling eyes rested back into his seat and Cecilia did the same. She needed to prepare for landing.

Cecilia couldn't focus on the unfamiliar place. She focused on finding Vi. The rental car didn't understand the urgency of its task and strained under Cecilia's demand. She pulled into Tubman Towers parking lot surprised at how difficult it would be to actually come face to face with her only child. Would her arms be enough? They hadn't been enough to stop Vi before. Somehow Cecilia would have to find the strength to make them enough. Tubman Towers was simply a maze Cecilia had to travel through to get to her child. She didn't notice 2Live Crew's lispy bravado, or the small clouds of talcum peppering the hall in front of the showers. Context was only background. 203D. The stark numbers felt out of place with the woman life permeating every nook and cranny of Tubman Tower. She pressed her knuckles against the door. Silence responded. She did it again. Still nothing.

Cecilia found the Attic like a mother-bear following the scent of her cub. A girl that could've been Vi sat in the bright subterranean room with her back toward the entrance. Cecilia exhaled. Vi was here, and she was whole. She touched her shoulder, but the face that turned to greet her didn't belong to her child. "I'm sorry I'm looking for Vi."

The girl barely covered a snarl. "Vi don't work here no more." She began pushing a cart toward the room's edges without looking back.

"What? When's the last time you saw her?"

The girl tossed a look over her shoulder and shrugged.

Cecilia closed the space between them in two steps. Her grip spun the girl 180 degrees. "Listen little girl. I'm going to ask you one more question. And you are going to look me in the eye and answer me like you have some sense. Is Dr. Locke here?"

The mask fell from her face, and the little unsure girl that had been hiding behind it emerged. "No. Ma'am. He doesn't work here anymore either. They got him up in Frenchtown Gardens. He can't even help himself."

Cecilia turned and headed back toward the door.

"You might want to check at the G-Nu house though. The Gamma Nu's. The boy she's…her boyfriend is a Gamma Nu."

Cecilia did not look back at the hiding girl. She ascended the stairs up to the library in a fog. Vi had a boyfriend she'd never mentioned. Someone who was more in her child's thoughts than she was or ever would be again.

The Gamma House was easy to find. Cecilia only had to follow the trail of testosterone. She rang the bell, but no one responded over the din of rap lyrics floating through every space in the wood frame exterior, so Cecilia abandoned the doorbell and began ramming her knuckles against the battered steel door.

Silence interrupted the blaring speakers and a voice boomed from behind the door. "Somebody Momma out there banging like the police. I'm not answering it."

Cecilia leaned into the door. "One of you better answer the door before I knock it down."

It opened suddenly. A young man in a shirt covered with Greek symbols blocked the door. "Sorry about that confusion ma'am. We had a long night. How can I help you?"

Cecilia strained to see past the symbols and the boy, but she couldn't. "I'm looking for a boy. He's dating my daughter, Vi Moon.

"Vi Moon? Oh? Perry's crazy baby momma? She carried him out of here a few days ago." Deep laughter pushed past the shorn man/boy in the door.

"What?" Cecilia blinked back the man/boy's meanness.

He tipped his head to one side, as if talking to someone of limited intelligence. "That crazy pregnant girl bought him at the auction and took him." He took a sip from the red plastic cup in his hand. "We haven't seen him since. If you find that mark, tell him he's on dishes detail."

Cecilia stepped up to deposit both her fear and rage onto this boy, but he seemed to anticipate her retribution, and the door closed. The testosterone-fueled noises within the confines of the man/boy sanctuary erupted again, and Cecilia backed off the porch onto the unkempt lawn.

"Mrs. Moon?"

Cecilia looked toward the white and silver stranger calling her by name. She wore her smile in the same way the girl from the Attic had worn her scorn, somewhere to hide.

"Mrs. Moon. I recognize you from Vi's picture." She extended her hand toward Cecilia. "I'm Danielle. The one who called."

Cecilia contemplated the well-manicured brown fingers on the pale callous-free palm attached to a wrist with a faint pyramid of ridges.

"Have you seen her?" They were all hiding from themselves, from each other, from their parents. Why had she sent her child to this place? So she could perfect her game of hide and seek?

"No. Not since the auction."

Was it really Vi those boys were talking about? "I've been to her dorm, to the Attic. Do you know anything about this Perry boy?"

Danielle shrugged. A frowning bald man/boy emerged from the house. "Dani. What's taking you so long?"

"I'm coming." The veil fell for a moment as she turned back toward Cecilia. She reached into her silver and white jacket. "When you find her can you give her this?" She placed a key in Cecilia's hand. "I'm moving in with my boyfriend." She paused before turning toward the house. "It's a lot cheaper than living on campus."

Did this child realize she wasn't her mother and didn't care who she lived with? All she cared about was decreasing the distance between herself and her child. "Is Vi pregnant?"

Danielle looked toward the man/boy still standing in the door.

"Is this Perry boy the father?"

She shrugged again. "Vi and me haven't been that close lately. I'm sorry Mrs. Moon. All I know I told you on the phone." She began to walk away. "She spends a lot of time in the Attic. Did you go there?"

Cecilia waved away her impotent suggestion. "How do I get to Frenchtown Gardens?"

A scent surrounded Frenchtown Gardens. It reminded Cecilia of when the summer cicadas descended on their block and Vi decided to cut into the heart of herself. Cecilia had to push herself across the threshold.

The smiling receptionist seemed more interested in the light following

Cecilia inside, than greeting her. Her eyes held the space between the closing door and its frame until it disappeared. Only then did she turn toward Cecilia. "Welcome to Frenchtown Gardens. Your Respite from the World." She said it the way people say things once meaning has separated from obligation.

"I'm here to see Dr. Locke." Cecilia was nervous and she didn't know why. The feeling she'd fought to control since Vi's birth bubbled into her chest like lava licking at the lips of a volcano.

"He'll be pleased. Please sign in." She whispered something into the phone. "Follow the cerulean stripe. He's in the Napoleon Room."

Cecilia found the blue line easily. Until, of course, the line changed to orange, or was it persimmon. If it hadn't, she would've kept walking. She welcomed a few seconds of following without thought, but she couldn't acquiesce control yet. She still had to find her child. She could feel that her first-born second-chance child was in real trouble.

He was easy to distinguish in the dim room. He sat alone, if you could call anyone sitting in the midst of hundreds of imagined worlds alone. A book lay open in his lap. His focused on a shelf lined with classics in front of him. He turned toward her as she entered.

"Dr. Locke?"

"Yes? Forgive me. I'm unable to distinguish your voice. Have we met?"

"No. I'm Cecilia Moon. Viola's mother."

"Ah. Ms. Moon's mother." His eyes moved to the twelve foot ceiling. "Is she with you?"

"No. Dr. Locke. I'm actually looking for her."

"Is she lost?"

Was she? Cecilia didn't not want to speak those words into the world. "   No."

"Mrs. Moon, please excuse my manners. Existing in such solitude tends to dull one's interpersonal competence. Please have a seat?"

Something about the way he looked through her without seeing unnerved Cecilia.

"Would you like something to drink? Water? Coffee? Tea?"

Cecilia shook her head, before realizing her body movements were indecipherable to this man. "No."

"You've come here for something more haven't you? I may not be able to see, but I'm not blind." He laughed.

Cecilia laughed with him and at herself. Maybe she was not as undecipherable as she believed. "I received a call from Vi's roommate. She told me some disturbing things and I haven't been able to reach Vi for a few days, so I thought it best I come down and see her face to face."

"So she is lost."

Cecilia squirmed in her seat. "She could just be off with friends for the weekend. She doesn't even know I'm here or looking for her."

"But your perspective is the only one that counts. Columbus didn't discover America from the native's perspective, yet we still close down all of our fine government institutions on his birthday. Perspective is fluid, yet fundamental, Mrs. Moon. And if you don't know where she is, then she is lost."

The lava climbed closer to the edge.

"And you need help finding her.   And you've come to me?"

"Yes. Dr. Locke. I need your help to find her."

"I'm sorry. I can't help you. I make it a practice not to foster personal relationships with my subordinates."

Cecilia failure didn't surprise her. Of course this was a long shot. Why would the man Vi worked for know where her child was? "Thank you Dr. Locke. I appreciate your time."

He laughed a bitter laugh. "My time. Mrs. Moon, time is all I have no matter how limited some may wish it." He pointed his eyes toward Cecilia's face. "You know your daughter has been my only visitor. That is before you. I believe I may have frightened her. When you find her, and rest assured that you will, please give her my sincere apologies. This place changes you in ways you can't imagine. Please tell her. Please tell her I look forward to seeing her again."

Cecilia leaned against the rental car no closer to finding Vi than she had been when she first answered Danielle's phone call. She reached for the keys to the car and pulled out the other one; the one Vi's roommate had given her. She should go back to Tubman Towers. Maybe Vi had returned, and all of this had been for nothing.

203D. The starkness of the numbers reflected the starkness of the room. A cell, consisting of the bare necessities of life. The only things that moved 203D beyond a chamber of incarceration were the books. There were so many. Different subjects; different authors; but one thing connected them all; Moon; authorship, subject, title, publication. The commonality stretched the limits of sameness. It must have taken her days, weeks to amass such a useless collection. What was she looking for? Cecilia approached Vi's desk. The lone scrap of celluloid hanging precariously on the bulletin board exacerbated her regret. Why had she sent her child here? Cecilia pulled out the pushpin. His face wasn't distinguishable. His eyes a memory. Is this it? Him? She had done everything in her power to erase him from both of their lives. It hadn't worked. She picked up the pillow on the bed, the only soft place in the room. Cecilia could smell Vi on it. Cecilia had pushed herself to the edges to make room for him at her center, and she wouldn't let Vi do the same. She'd hoped Vi was young enough to forget her father. Not so much forget him, but who Cecilia became when she was with him. She wanted Vi to forget the way Cecilia walked on tiptoe and talked in hushed tones around him. The ways she anticipated his needs before he needed. Cecilia hoped Vi had forgotten all the ways she'd stuffed her truth into a box each day, just to have that box explode each night.

She would have to find the boy. If she found Perry, she would find Vi.

She let the rental car idle across the street as she watched the house. She had sent her away to avoid this; to stop a reincarnation. Cecilia needed Vi to be ahead of her, not behind her. After an hour the girl and the man/boy she was moving in with exited the house. "Danielle."

The girl stopped, but the boy kept walking. "Mrs. Moon? You still haven't found her?"

Cecilia shook her head. "Is there anyone else that may know where she is? A friend?"

Danielle shook her head before her face lit up. "Vi did have a friend.

He left last semester though, so I don't know if he would be any help. Ronnie. Ronnie Tredway." She turned toward the man/boy leaning against a car. "Ju, isn't Ronnie Tredway your homeboy."

"Ronnie who?"

"You know Ronnie Tredway. The one who left after that stuff with Dr. Bennett."

He raised his head. "I know of him. I don't know know him. But yeah. His people from Quincy."

"Do you know where they stay?"

He blew out as if exasperated. "What you trying to say? Me and homeboy wasn't tight like that."

"Ju, this is important. Everybody knows where everybody lives in Quincy."

When he pulled himself off of the car and began walking toward them, Cecilia knew without knowing that she would find her second-chance child.

The house reminded Cecilia of something she'd forgotten. A place she'd visited once when she still had a family. It was the kind of house generations would get to enjoy, meant for both the past and future. Her footsteps echoed up the pine steps. Sounds of a whirring fan and forgotten radio seeped through the screen door. "Hello." Her voice floated back unanswered, so she walked around the back of the house. A woman, bent uneasily over a vine heavy with green tomatoes, collected them carefully in her apron.

"Hello."

The woman looked up without surprise. "Hey there." She struggled a bit to stand, and Cecilia quickened her steps to offer her arm. Warmth spread across the woman's face. "How you?"

"Hot."

"Well. Yes there's always that." She removed her hat and fanned herself with it before placing it back onto her head. "I try to wait until the sun is on its way down before I come out here, but it don't seem to matter much. I just all of a sudden got me a taste for some green tomatoes. You like fried tomatoes?"

Cecilia nodded.

She gestured for Cecilia to follow her. She walked over to a towering blue spruce and the seat swing nestled under it. "Seem like these tomatoes was begging me to pick them." She brushed dirt from them as they sat easily in her lap. "They gone make a real nice supper tonight. You welcome to stay … Oh I'm sorry I can't recall your name."

"I'm sorry Mrs. Tredway. I never gave it to you. I'm Cecilia. Cecilia Moon."

She laughed as if she'd been caught. "Okay Cecilia. You know how it is. Memory is not what it used to be, and you look like I may have seen you before. You can call me Esther. Now I don't guess you came all the way out here in this heat to hear me go on about my dinner plans."

"Actually I'm looking for Ronnie."

Esther turned in her seat. "Ronnie?"

"Well really I'm looking for my daughter, Vi. I haven't talked to her in awhile, and I was hoping Ronnie could help me find her."

"Oh you're little Ms. Viola's mother." She looked closer at Cecilia. "That's where I know you from. Should have known it when I saw you. She has your eyes."

Cecilia smiled.

"But I don't know if Ronnie will be able to help you. He's up in Atlanta. Been there since November. Tried to keep him close, but they wasn't ready for my baby up at A&M."

"Esther. Were Vi and Ronnie seeing each other?"

Esther giggled sweetly. "No Baby. They wasn't seeing each other. At least not in the way you mean. They sure did love each other though."

"How can you be so sure? If they loved each other as much as you say they did, then…"

"Ronnie don't like girls. I mean at least in the way you mean." She dusted the tomatoes as she spoke.

"Oh, I'm sorry."

"Nothing to be sorry about. Ronnie just the way he is. He's just fine." She looked back toward the house. "You want to come in the house while I give him a call for you."

Cecilia shook her head and leaned back on the bench. "I'll wait here if you don't mind."

Cecilia watched as Esther carried her tomatoes in the house, cradling them with both hands careful not to crush them. Is that what she had done to Vi? Held her too tight? Is that why Vi was... Was she damaged or just fine like Ronnie? Either way Cecilia couldn't shake the feeling if she didn't find her child soon she might be lost to her forever. Cecilia barely noticed Esther's return.

"He hasn't heard from her since he left, but he said he'd call right away if he did." She placed her hand on Cecilia's. "Sometimes these children need to get away from us. They need to separate to decide what kind of men or women they're going to be. I wouldn't worry if I was you. That child will be back safe and sound before you know it."

Maybe Esther was right. Maybe this thing Vi was going through, whatever it was, she needed to go through on her own. As Cecilia drove away from the house, she couldn't help thinking that somehow she was leaving more than just a plate of fried green tomatoes behind.

CHAPTER TWENTY

She knew she'd arrived in Elysia even without the overly friendly signs that bid her hello and goodbye in the last ten towns she drove through. They stopped at the only gas station on the road to ask for directions to the address she got from the pieces of hate Diana had flung at her. The old man behind the counter smiled slow at her request as if directing lost daughters home was his sole occupation. Vi turned off the main highway onto a narrow steep dirt road. Blue Thunder squealed with a strained determination followed by a cloud of red dust. They passed two or three turnoffs before she matched the route number to the one on the paper, turned onto an even steeper narrower road. When she reached the top, the trees accompanying their climb up the mountain disappeared, leaving an exposed uneven patch of red earth. At the center of the broad patch of clay, sat a mobile home that had seen better days. A dusty ancient Packard sat on milk crates on the side of the trailer. They exited the car, and she stretched. She'd been driving for hours, and recognized the pressure on her bladder as she climbed the stairs leading up to the trailer's front door. Snippets of a television game show traveled through the screen's perforations.

The shadow of the well-used screen blocked the full detail of the man.

"I'm looking for Ellington Moon."

He stepped closer and into view.

"I'm Viola."

He opened the door and squinted back the sun shining into his face. A slow recognition pushed his eyes wide open despite the glare. "My Viola. My Viola." He whispered it as he motioned for her to enter.

Too scared to look directly at him, like the sun during an eclipse, Vi focused on the room, a creolisation of worlds. Handmade blankets with wide stripes of red, black, and green covered a floral print settee that looked as if it had come straight from an English parlor. Four cane back chairs surrounded a simple pine table. A British colonialist desk sat under carvings from Nigeria. Pieces of colorful silk were draped over kente cloth at each window. She leaned back into the homemade red, black and green blanket on the back of the settee, as the child struggled for breath at her feet.

"Do you remember me?" His soft face temporarily morphed into something harder, trying to recreate a younger and slimmer jawline.

Did she remember? Vi mentally filed through the dreams she dreamed and redreamed and none of them revealed any parts of this doughy man and his eclectic taste. Was this what she had been searching through the bowels of Woodson's Library for? She didn't have the heart to tell him the truth. "Yes."

He reminded her of Ronnie. "Me and your mother brought you down here when you was still knee high to caterpillar. You loved it here."

This place felt as foreign to Vi as the man sitting across from her. "Did we live here?"

"No. no. Don't really live here now. Just stopping through. This is my father's land."

She had a father, and he had a father. This was their land. She had been right. She was not a nigger. She had people. She wanted to ask him to tell her everything, but she was afraid her hunger, like the child's, would overwhelm him, so she allowed silence to engulf them both.

"You look just like your mother."

She couldn't remember a time when anyone had compared her to Cecilia in any way. But as she caught his eye, she realized his eyes weren't hers.

A woman too young to have interfered with their life Before came into the house.

"This is my wife, Liberia. Liberia this is my daughter."

"Hello." Her face held all the hardness that his lacked. "You staying?

Vi didn't know what to say. Even if there had been welcome in the woman's voice, she knew she couldn't stay here. She lied, recalling one of the towns she passed through to get to Elysia. "I have a hotel room over in Anniston. Prepaid. Couldn't get my money back if I wanted to."

Liberia nodded, and her face softened. It seems Vi answered correctly. The new wife disappeared down the narrow dark hall into the back of the trailer.

The baby's gasps for air became more pronounced. Vi's discovery of her people had in no way revived her. It seemed the trip had been for naught. He was either unable or too late to feed her. Vi opened her mouth, then closed it. She wanted to get her father's attention, but couldn't push the word daddy past her lips. "Ellington. I probably should be going. "

He seemed to notice her discomfort. "I want to show you something, before you go."

Even though she knew the child's time was short, they followed him out of the door as the sun was just starting to give way to the evening.

Ellington spoke of his history, somehow knowing what she'd come for. First the rusty old Packard in the yard. It had been his father's and now it was his. He planned to get it running again and then it would be Vi's if she wanted it. Did she want it? A low moan escaped from the child, and a sharp pain moved through Vi's lower back.

"Do you need to rest?"

"No." She said. "It's just the baby."

"Of course." He leaned against the trunk of a red oak and waited. "We're almost there."

When they reached the four-way stop, the church stood out of the center of the trees like a beacon, clearly designed for function, not form, a sensible structure. The church's exterior walls had been painted the color of the sun at some point, but time had faded it into something much less brilliant.

"What's this?

"Our church."

Confusion flashed across her face. Our. She'd never been in this place. How could it belong to her?

He clarified, "Moons."

Of course, he had said we, she was a Moon. They were a collective. She was a part.

So this was it. The holy ground. The place she should've known without asking. Vi waited to feel some sort of connection to this place.

In between the child's gasps, she waited for a flash of lightning, rattling of thunder, for the heavens to open up and rain down on both of them, healing her mind and the child's body. She reached out and held the child's hand for the first time. It was the first time she'd actually touched her out of anything but necessity. The baby fat had melted away into nothing. Her once pudgy fingers felt like dry twigs.

Ellington was saying something about his daddy's daddy or granddaddy, but Vi couldn't focus. The child could no longer move on her accord, so Vi lifted her into her arms. As the child laid her head against Vi's shoulder, she noticed a small patch of cleared land to the left of the church. "What's that?"

He puffed up with what looked to be pride, but Vi no longer trusted her own perception. "Family cemetery." He began moving in that direction, so she followed with the child in her arms.

"Three generations of Moon's right here. My father, his father, and his father. My brother is there, and this is my uncle."

So this would be the child's final resting place. It all started to make sense. Vi couldn't have imagined a more poetic ending. She was meant to find this man and this place because the baby was supposed to be buried here. "Where's Viola Moon? I don't see her."

"You're standing on her; breathing her."

"What?"

"Cremated and scattered. All of them are everywhere."

Vi scanned the headstones for names signifying a female ancestor. "You mean all the women?"

He nodded as if cremation was better: an honor bestowed only on the women. Was it an honor to not be recorded? Ellington seemed to think so. Another pain radiated through her lower back. She bent over and the child tumbled from her arms into the dust. Vi dropped to her knees, attempting to gather the child up in her arms, but it was too late. The child was dead.

"Are you okay?   The baby?"

"No. Neither one of us is okay." Vi assessed the headstones again. There was no place for either of them here. "Ellington I need to go."

"Don't you want to rest for awhile before getting back on the road?"

"I'm fine. I just need to be getting back before it gets dark."

This was an excuse he could not argue with. These narrow unlit roads were not kind to strangers, especially after sundown.

The child proved to be heavier in death than life. In life she had followed, but now Vi had no choice but to carry her. As Vi struggled under the weight, a need for a concrete answer blossomed in her chest. "Why did you leave us?"

His mouth narrowed, and he moved the dirt of his foremothers in a circle with his foot. "She kept telling me to."

Vi shook her head. "Cecilia told me one day she woke up and you were gone.

He nodded. "She would tell me to leave in her sleep. In the morning she would never remember saying it, but I couldn't forget hearing it. So one morning I did what she couldn't bring herself to ask me to do in the light of the day.

Vi began to walk away and then stopped. "What about the first baby?"

His eyebrows moved together. "What?

"The baby she had before me."

"Vi you are our only child. Cecilia didn't have any children before you."

Vi looked down at the child she carried. Who was this if not Cecilia's first child? Whose first chance was she carrying? Hot tears ran down Vi's face as she picked up her pace. The clearing where she'd left Blue Thunder was right ahead.

"Slow down Viola. You have to think about your baby."

She gently lay the baby in the back seat, wiping the tears away, leaving thick bands of dust down both sides of her face. "She's all I ever think about."

HWY 90 was a lonely road. Blue Thunder crept along, headed out of Elysia back to where? A sign pointing toward Quincy grew up out of the cattails lining the side of the road. She made the turn without thinking. She pushed the gas pedal to the floor, and let Elysia disappear from her rearview window.

The pain rode over her in waves. Each one longer than the last. The problem before her, both new and old. Old: what do with the child? New: what to do with the dead child? Vi tried not to look at the emaciated and limp representation of the baby's former self in the back seat. She had to find a place for her; a place where girl children were not burned and discarded; a place where walls were not only designated for carriers of the familial name. She didn't want this child to be forgotten again. She sped down Hwy 19 until she reached the unmarked and familiar road. She sped by Crazy Mary's shack. Were those flowers always there? She passed Big Ron's and Miss Esther's house up on the hill. The road ended before they reached the red oak. The pain radiating down the small of her back continued like the ebb and flow of lake Michigan banging against the shore in the Spring. She managed to get the child out of the car and headed for the cemetery. Just as she would brace herself against the shooting pain it would ease, and they could move forward. It felt like hours, because the respites were getting shorter. She bit down on her tongue to keep from screaming. Night had fallen and the cool breeze made carrying the child and the pain easier. By the time she'd entered the gates of Ronnie's ancestral resting place, the ebb and flow had given way to constant pain. She wanted to squat and ease the pressure, but she had to bury the child first. She laid the child's body at the foot of the oak and crawled to a soft patch of unmarked earth. She had nothing but her hands, so she began to dig. The urge to squat overwhelmed her, but she didn't stop digging. She'd managed to carve a large enough space in the soil to place the child in it face up. The baby looked so peaceful that Vi hesitated to cover her. She placed the paper, the one that Diana had thrown at her as proof of her peoplelessness, over the baby's face before replacing the soil. The rest of the plots had markings. She needed to find something to mark the grave with. The pain cut her off from her own thoughts. Something inside of her needed to come out, and no matter how hard she tried to render it invisible it was going to be seen. But all she needed now was a headstone. A way to mark this body as belonging to her, but pain and sound cut through her need. She squatted and pushed.

"Baby, Are you okay?"

It was a voice all at once known and unknown. Cecilia. Now she had moved past imagining the imaginary. Now she was imagining the real. "Are you real?'

The sound and sight combined as Cecilia knelt in the dirt next to her. "You aren't real. This is not real."

Cecilia laughed a laugh that was all at once familiar and not. "Of course this is really me." Cecilia's face faded and a woman with Ronnie's face came into focus, and Vi could see who she wasn't.

"Crazy Mary?"

She snorted in response. "My friends just call me Mary. What do yours call you?"

"Vi."

"Vi, can you walk?"

The pain bent her over in response.

"I'm going to go see if there's something softer in the car for you to rest on."

Vi could hear footsteps moving away and coming back just as another sharp pain shot up the back of her spine, forcing her to the ground.

"Here you go. It ain't much, but it's going to have to do. Lean back and rest your head on this." Mary kneeled between Vi's legs, spreading them wide.

"Ms. Mary, I'm scared. I'm not ready."

Mary looked between her legs and patted Vi's knee. "If we waited until we was ready, wouldn't be no babies born ever.

The pressure between her legs suddenly increased. "I need to push again."

Mary nodded. "Go head then."

Vi pushed with everything she had been holding onto. She pushed as if expelling every pretense and secret, and the pain eased. And just like that, the thing she couldn't see before suddenly existed in the flesh.

This child cried out in a way Vi wasn't accustomed to. It sounded nothing like the cry of the child she'd just buried. Mary placed the baby against Vi's breast and guided the child's rooting lips onto Vi's breast. And in that moment, the screams of hunger that haunted Vi for months were displaced by the rhythm of a contented suckling.

Mary touched the child's head. "What you gone call her?"

"What?"

"Her name baby. What's her name?"

The small mound of fresh dirt stood only a few feet away from her. Vi shook her head. She could finally see her. Naming seemed insignificant. A soft cooing emanated from the little girl in her arms, and both breasts began to fill. The edges of the question around her heart softened as sign separated from the signified and left only sound.

EPILOGUE

Lana made such a fuss over the tub. She wanted running water. She didn't want the work of her childhood. As children, they had been forced to move the water from the well to the tub like mules. Only one bath every 2 weeks because of the trouble, then the sharing of the bath between all of them. Washing in the filth of other's was worse than not washing at all. So he made sure she got her tub, and her children would know the luxury of both daily and singular baths. They would not have to stew in the stink of others. They would wash alone.

"I'm clean mommy." Cecilia managed to splash more water on the bathroom floor than in the tub.

"That's Enough Cecilia. I've told you ten times already. Out of the tub. You're getting water everywhere?"

"Please. Second chance. Mommy. Please." She balled up her chubby cheeks in the way Lana had never been able to resist.

"Okay Cecie. Second chance. But then we're going to have to empty the tub for Baby Violet."

Cecilia continued to splash in the water until the suds were a foam on the surface. She pulled the plug and watched the water turn into a swirl at the center of the spout, her favorite part of the bath. "Mommy. Where does the water go?"

"Somewhere deep under the city, and out into the lake. Now let's run the water for the baby."

"Baby Violet's turn?"

"Yes. Cecie. It's baby's turn." Lana grabbed the baby from the playpen. She was as fat and as beautiful as Cecilia. Everyone always commented on how they had made two beautiful girls. She placed the baby in the tub, and began to run the water. Was that the bell ringing? Had he forgotten his key again? The bell rang again. This time more persistently. She pushed herself up from her knees and twisted the water spigot off. "Cecie, keep an eye on baby sister while momma let's Daddy in."

"Okay Momma." Cecilia kneeled next to the tub, and began to blow bubbles at her little sister.

Lana fussed as she went to the front door. "Why do you keep forgetting your key? This is starting to get…"

The man on the other side of the door wasn't her man at all. He wore a grin and carried a briefcase, selling something that she neither needed or wanted. Just as she was going to tell him, her Cecilia interrupted.

"Momma. Come see. Baby sister is in the water."

"Of course she is Cecie. Keep and eye on her for me. No splashing. Okay."

"Okay?"

She watched Cecilia skip back toward the bathroom. Her hestiation must have given the salesman of nothing she wanted or needed renewed hope, because he restarted his sales pitch with new vigor.

By the time she closed the door, Lana could hear running water and splashing from the bathroom. She moved quickly toward the front door. A small stream of water met her in the hallway. She was sure she closed the spigot before she'd gone to the door. But when she opened the bathroom door the water had flowed over the edges of the tub. At first Lana thought it was a doll Cecilia had placed in the tub for Baby Violet to play with. But as she focused, and then refocused she realized it wasn't a doll at all.

Lana moved in slow motion when she lifted the lifeless body of Baby Violet out of the water, and held her to her chest.

"Don't cry Mommy. I'm sorry. Baby Violet wanted bubbles. Don't cry. Second chance. Please."

Lana wanted to scream, but the only thing that kept coming to her head was the fuss she made over having running water.

Acknowledgments

Viola's story has had many manifestations, readers, supporters and critics since I completed the first draft back in 2003. This small part of her story would've never been fully realized without the support of many.

I'd like to thank my guides.
I'm grateful to Sandra Jackson Opoku, my sister-teacher, whose vision of what this could be helped me to push it past where it began. Thank you to the Chicago State University M.F.A. faculty Kelly Norman Ellis, Haki Madhubuti, and Sterling Plump. You have each inspired, encouraged, and listened as I battled through the rigors of real life to find a space to build an imagined life. Thank you to ZZ Packer, Tayari Jones, Mat Johnson, and David Haynes. Your work and feedback have been crucial in my development as a writer and a teacher.

I'd like to thank my writing communities, past and present.
The Gwendolyn Brooks Writers Collective, the Writers and Wine Workshop, and the Voices of Chicago Literati. Specifically, I'd like to thank Barbara Thomas, Crystal Wiley, Bryant Smith, Audrey Tolliver, Janine Harrison Poore, Dawn Liddicoat, and Shannon Monroe for reading and rereading Vi's story in many of its incarnations.

I'd like to thank the Kimbilio Center for Fiction, Voices of Our Nation Writers Workshop, Callaloo Writers Workshop, Vermont Studio Center, and the Noepe Center for Literary Arts for giving me the space and time to complete what I started at my dining room table so many years ago.

I'd like to thank my parents, Elizabeth and Clinton Lavalais, for giving me permission to mine our familial history for inspiration and encouraging me on this journey.

To my children Etienne and Tia Martinez, thank you for understanding (mostly) that turning empty pages into a novel, though it requires a little magic, mostly takes time.

Thank you Heather Buchanan and Willow Books for working so hard to bring this project to fruition and being a beacon for emerging and established writers of color. And to the coolest cat in the business, my editor Randall Horton, thank you for your thoughtful edits and unrelenting encouragement throughout this process. You rock both literally and figuratively.

To my publicist Kima Jones of Jack Jones Literary Arts, I can't thank you enough for believing and fighting for this project when even I was ready to throw in the towel. You are truly a force to be reckoned with.

To my husband, Steve Martinez, thank you for supporting me in every way a human being can possibly support another human being. I have leaned on you emotionally, financially, and physically throughout this journey, and you have never ever faltered.

About the Author

Cole Lavalais received her MFA in Creative Writing from Chicago State University. She has been awarded writer's residencies at the Vermont Studio Center and The Noepe Center for the Literary Arts. An inaugural fellow of the Kimbilio Center for Fiction, Cole's short stories have appeared in several print and online literary journals. Cole hosts the Voices of Chicago's Literati Salon (a salon featuring writers of color) and teaches community-based writing workshops on the south side of Chicago. She is currently at work on her second novel.

CPSIA information can be obtained at www.ICGtesting.com
Printed in the USA
LVOW08s0805100716

495744LV00008B/339/P

9 780996 139045